JUMPING THE SHARK

Paranormal Talent Agency

Episode Five

HEATHER SILVIO

Panther Books

Published in the United States by Panther Books, Las Vegas.

Correspondence to the author may be sent to:
heather@heathersilvio.com

Cover design by Sonia Freitas at Chloe Belle Arts
https://ChloeBelleArts.com

ISBN (Print) 978-1-7326938-7-6
ISBN (E-book) 978-1-7326938-8-3

BOOKS BY HEATHER SILVIO

PARANORMAL TALENT AGENCY

Lights, Camera, Action (Episode One)

Reset to One (Episode Two)

That's a Wrap (Episode Three)

An Unexpected Sequel (Episode Four)

Jumping the Shark (Episode Five)

The Season Finale (Episode Six)

NON-SERIES FICTION

Not Quite Famous: A Romantic Comedy of an Actress
on the Edge

Beyond the Abyss: Tales of the Supernatural

Courting Death

NONFICTION

Special Snowflake Syndrome: The Unrecognized
Personality Disorder Destroying the World

Happiness by the Numbers: 9 Steps to Authentic
Happiness

Stress Disorders: A Healing Path for PTSD

ACKNOWLEDGMENTS

Thank you to my author groups for their guidance on writing a series!

CHAPTER ONE

Humanity drove me bananas; how hard was it to do what a demon wanted? I glanced at the humans surrounding me. They seemed so excited to support my bid for Mayor, after my years representing them on the city council. Of course, they didn't know I was a demon.

Tonight was a big night for all of us – the final debate before the primary elections in only one week. I was hanging out with my campaign volunteers to show my thanks for their support, but the metal folding chairs in campaign headquarters were uncomfortable. Who ordered these wretched things?

"Barbara, we'll be getting on the bus in about an hour. Need to leave in thirty minutes."

The voice interrupted my pointless wandering thoughts and I focused on the young woman standing before me, brown eyes wide behind bright red glasses. "Thank you,

Lynn." I stood and stretched my arms to the side. Taking the form of a middle-aged human somehow brought aches and pains with it. Not cool. "I'll be in my office. Please come get me when it's time."

"Yes, ma'am." Lynn Fox, my campaign manager, walked away and I watched her confer with two volunteers. I smiled at the volunteers I passed on my way to my office, and closed the door firmly behind me. And sighed. I understood why they wanted the candidates to arrive together; it made for a better visual. On the other hand, that meant extra travel time to meet the bus.

Unlike in campaigns past, this debate had importance. There were four challengers for the position. I normally wouldn't care, except that, for the supernatural, the head of the city council is also usually the ruler of the underworld. I'd been the unofficial head of the city council because the current mayor was a human, and an idiot. But he was stepping down. I couldn't risk a supernatural taking his place who might not want to recognize the existing power structure. I wasn't planning on giving up my status as Ruler of the Supernatural Underworld.

One of the challengers was a popular local actor, Jeffrey Jenkins. He'd been getting a lot of press lately. That made me nervous, though I still expected to be victorious. It was my destiny. I sighed again. I needed to do well in the debate tonight to solidify my position. Polls showed the two of us running neck and neck, with a fellow supernatural a close third. He was an interesting one, Mark Mammon. Though I hadn't met him yet.

A mist swirled before me and I braced myself. The mist existed only in my mind, and signaled an impending premonition. I closed my eyes and waited. My mind's eye showed me the bus for the debate tonight. Hmm. As future me walked toward the bus, movement became tortured. I trudged forward, fighting against the feeling of walking through molasses, knowing I needed to get on that bus. It became too difficult. Future me stopped fighting and froze, a weight lifted. I watched the bus doors close and the bus drive away. Part of me felt like I should call after it; I couldn't not get on the bus. I needed to be at the debate. But, future me felt relieved.

Present me snapped her eyes open in the office. The premonition was over. Now to figure out what it meant. I tapped my fingers on the plastic folding table before me. This could be tricky.

Everything had fallen apart in the past three months. After literally hundreds of years of accurate premonitions, things had become wonky. Only a few months ago, even my minion had been able to break her pact with me. I narrowed my eyes at the thought of Robin Landon's cheekiness. My premonitions hadn't breathed a word of that betrayal. More importantly, I'd had a premonition that a witch, Jackson McKee – Robin's new boyfriend (hard eye roll at that thought) – was involved in a loss of my power, but I'd been unsuccessful in eliminating him. As I admitted to Robin in our last encounter, my precognition was on the fritz. What other explanation could there be for these outcomes?

Thus, my current dilemma. My premonition suggested I shouldn't get on the bus. Could that be the wrong interpretation? Or maybe the premonition was wrong entirely. I ground my teeth together. A soft knock on the door drew my attention. Lynn poked her head in.

"It's time, Ms. Knollman."

I frowned and did not stand.

"Sorry. Barbara." When I still didn't respond, Lynn matched my frown. "Is everything okay?"

"Yes. I won't be taking the debate bus," I declared, decision made.

Her mouth dropped open for a moment before she recovered. "I'll inform the coordinator." She closed the door. At least she knew better than to question me.

Now to see what happened.

CHAPTER TWO

A ding signaled an incoming text message. 702 area code, but not a number I knew. I lifted a single eyebrow at the message on the phone's screen.

Hi Barbara. This is Mark. You didn't get on the bus.

Curious. *No.*

Turn on the news.

"Lynn, turn the television to Channel 5," I instructed my campaign manager. We were in a limo heading to the debate, which was set to start in twenty minutes. The television clicked on and Lynn scrolled. Elizabeth Addison's sorrowful face filled the small screen on the back of the car seat.

"I'm at the scene of a horrific accident," the newscaster said. "About fifteen minutes ago, the bus carrying the mayoral candidates to their final debate crashed. Details remain hazy, but it appears there were no survivors."

Lynn gasped.

I listened for the approximate location of the crash, muted the broadcast, and lowered the divider between us and the driver.

"There's been an accident involving the debate bus. Please head toward DI and Las Vegas Boulevard. Get as close to the accident as you can."

"Yes, ma'am."

I raised the divider and unmuted the broadcast. Elizabeth stood a block from the accident. Flashing lights illuminated much of what was behind her. A bus lay on its side, front crumpled like a soda can.

You weren't on the bus either.

I wondered what Mark's response to my text would be. I listened to Elizabeth's continued coverage while I waited.

The brunette broadcaster put a hand to her ear, probably trying to isolate a voice coming through her earpiece. "I've just been informed that the Sheriff has arrived on scene." Elizabeth nodded at the camera and then turned to sprint toward the accident. The image returned to an anchor in-studio and I muted the broadcast again. I'd wait until they had more information. My mind was spinning with what I'd already learned.

A bus crashed that I was supposed to be on. A bus crash that my premonition saved me from.

Why?

Mark Mammon also wasn't on the bus.

The camera returned to Elizabeth standing next to the tall, gray-haired Sheriff. His city had seen some rough stuff since he won election. He looked at least a decade older than he had when he'd taken office. Such were the perils of power.

I unmuted the broadcast.

"What can you tell us?"

"The last body has been pulled from the wreckage. At this time, I can confirm three of the five candidates—"

"Which candidates?" Elizabeth interrupted, but given Mark's text, I knew.

"—along with three staff members," the Sheriff continued without acknowledging her question, "and the bus driver, have been killed."

"What happened?"

"The cause of the accident is unknown, though witnesses report the bus did not seem to slow as it crested Desert Inn toward the Las Vegas Boulevard traffic light."

"Does the department believe this was a terrorist attack?"

"We have no reason to believe that at this time," the Sheriff concluded, smiled tightly at viewers, and turned to hurry away from the reporter.

I doubted it was a terrorist attack either. I also doubted it was just an accident.

My limo had nearly arrived at the intersection of the accident when Mark responded.

And then there were two.

I chuckled at the audacity. I guessed that confirmed what Elizabeth had reported. He and I were the only candidates remaining. Seemed only fitting, since we were the two paranormal beings. Both demons, in fact. I thinned my lips in thought. This begged two very important questions.

It seemed unlikely, but did Mark not know I was a demon?

And, I had my premonition warning me away from the bus; how did Mark know not to board the bus?

CHAPTER THREE

The slowing of the limo and the sound of the divider lowering pulled me from my thoughts. I made eye contact with the driver in the rearview mirror.

"Ma'am, we've arrived."

He didn't have to specify where. The lights from emergency vehicles pierced the limo's window tint, and controlled chaos ruled the scene.

"Good luck," Lynn offered.

I paused in opening my door. Sarcastic or sincere? Maybe I could play nice for a bit until I figured out what was going on. I smiled wide at her. "Thank you." I exited the vehicle and took in the scene before me.

Controlled chaos was definitely an accurate description. I counted five ambulances. No, wait, six. Three firetrucks and five police vehicles scattered around the debate bus, indeed lying on its side, front end crumpled. I spotted

Elizabeth and her cameraman, still shooting live coverage, and headed in her direction.

Elizabeth's eyes lit up when she saw me. She recognized a scoop when she saw it. "Councilwoman, why weren't you on the bus?" Her shouted question reached me.

I did not respond. Yelling across the space between us wasn't dignified. And I was the head of the city council after all.

She wisely did not repeat her question and simply watched me approach.

"Good evening, Ms. Addison. I'm happy to answer any questions that you have."

"Why weren't you on the bus?"

"A last-minute change of plans resulted in my choosing to drive myself to the debate."

"Well, technically, you have a limo."

A pulse throbbed in my neck. "Yes, you are correct. What I meant to say was that my campaign arranged private transportation when it was decided I wouldn't be taking the bus."

"And what were these last-minute plans that kept you from the bus?"

Like a dog with a bone. "Confidential campaign activities."

"That's convenient."

"Are you insinuating that I had anything to do with this crash, Ms. Addison?"

She winced at my sharp tone and her cheeks flushed. She knew I called her bluff. "Of course not. I'm only asking what my viewers will be wondering. How did you know not to get on the bus?"

I paused as if collecting my thoughts. I wasn't about to mention I had a premonition, but I needed to nip this in the bud. "I had no advance knowledge that anything was going to happen to the bus. Of course, I didn't. There was no nefarious reason I wasn't on board. I am as shocked and devastated as the rest of Las Vegas at this senseless accident and loss of life."

"Maybe not quite as devastated, though, right?"

I remained silent, hyper-aware of the camera likely zoomed in on my face, waiting for any micro-reaction.

"After all, now there are only two candidates for your position," she finished triumphantly.

I allowed a half-smile to surface. "Ms. Addison, I have every confidence that I will win this election. Neither myself, nor Mark Mammon, who also was not on the bus tonight, wanted the race to be reduced through such means."

I saw the internal calculations play out across Elizabeth's face. The Sheriff hadn't told her who the other surviving candidate was. Like me, she was considering what Mark might know or not know about the bus crash.

"My thoughts and prayers go out to the victims of tonight's crash, as well as their friends and family. Thank you." With that, I walked away. Elizabeth shouted something, her words lost on the wind that picked that moment to blow harsher. I hurried to the limo. The door tried to slip from my grasp but I was able to hold it open long enough to slip inside.

"Are you okay?"

The broadcast continued on the screen behind her and I assumed she watched my interview. It could have been better. It could have been worse. I shrugged. "I'm fine." I lowered the partition. "Please bring me to my office."

"Yes, ma'am."

I raised the partition and faced Lynn. "I'll head to work for a bit, in case there's anything requiring my immediate attention. We should assume for now that the next week will involve minimal continued campaigning."

Lynn nodded and whipped out her cellphone. I turned my attention inward as her fingers flew across the device, probably alerting anybody who needed to know that I would be laying low for the time being. I was savvy enough to understand I didn't want it to appear I was taking advantage of the tragedy. Although, Mark was correct.

Only two candidates remained.

CHAPTER FOUR

I drummed my fingernails on my solid wood monstrosity of a desk. In between providing soundbites to other members of the media concerning the tragedy, I reviewed the papers scattered across the surface of the desk. Once the final candidates had filed their paperwork, I'd hired a private investigator to dig up everything they could on the other four. The actor had been the biggest obvious threat. The two nobodies were exactly that. I set aside their dossiers and opened the one remaining.

Mark Mammon. I'd hired a supernatural private investigator because I'd assumed at least one of the other candidates would be supernatural. I'd been right. The investigator had struggled to follow the leads on Mr. Mammon. I wasn't surprised once the preliminary information came in; he was a demon like me and we weren't exactly known for wanting to share that.

Mark was older than my 500 years, but the trail of personas ran cold at about 750 years. He could be 1000 years old, for all I knew. That was worrisome because he may or may not be stronger as a result. I placed his picture on top of the pile.

Devilishly handsome man. I chuckled at my wit. Thick black hair, depthless black eyes that pulled at you. High cheekbones and a strong chin rounded out his striking features. Could be Greek or Roman, with that profile.

I laughed aloud when I considered his name. The name Mark meant God of War. And Mammon was a higher-level demon who evoked greed and deceit. So, a greedy demon starting war. Someone like that might crash a debate bus. Someone like that most certainly could want to rule the supernatural underworld.

Here I pursed my lips in thought. Although a large region, Las Vegas wasn't the biggest region to rule. Why was Mark here, trying to snatch my rule from me? Wouldn't he want to go after New York City, or one of the bigger regions in Europe maybe? I gnashed my teeth in frustration. What was his end game?

My cellphone rang. I frowned at it for a moment before answering. "Barbara Knollman speaking."

"Ms. Knollman, this is Detective Jacob Dawson, with the Las Vegas Police Department."

I rolled my eyes; I was well aware of the owner of the gruff voice. Although just a human, he was involved with

Mia Fynn, a fellow supernatural allied with the Paranormal Talent Agency. "What can I do for you, Detective?"

"I'd like to schedule a time to speak with you regarding the bus crash that occurred earlier tonight."

No preamble. He probably saw my interview with Elizabeth. I wasn't keen on being interviewed by him, but perhaps I could gain my own knowledge. While I knew I had nothing to do with the accident, it was very likely someone, maybe Mark, was involved. Perhaps I could pull some of that information from the detective.

"Ma'am? Are you there?"

"Sorry, I was reviewing my schedule in my head." The lie rolled easily off my tongue. "How about tomorrow at 9? Would you like me to come to the station?" I offered only to appear agreeable. He and I both knew I wouldn't be coming down to the station.

"That's not necessary, ma'am. I'll come to you. Thank you."

"You're most welcome, Detective. I'll see you in the morning." I ended the call and leaned back in the overstuffed dark leather chair. Now this was a comfortable chair. Why couldn't I have gotten one like this for at least my campaign headquarters office?

I turned my attention back to the dossier for Mark Mammon, although there was little left to review. The list of names he'd used, going back 750 years. Interestingly, he almost always used a variant of Mark — such as Marc,

Markus, Marcus — and a surname with a deeper meaning. Maybe my demon competitor possessed unknown depths?

I laughed and my eyes burned. If anyone had been in the room, they would have seen the unearthly red glow emanating from them. I didn't actually care whether or not Mark had depth. I needed to find out if he caused the bus crash and if he'd really been so insolent as to have tried to kill me.

CHAPTER FIVE

My dark house beckoned. I maneuvered the Cadillac Escalade – black of course – onto the driveway of my two-story abode. I lived in the Las Vegas Country Club Estates, not because I cared about being on a golf course, but because of the implied prestige and the wheeling-and-dealing I'd done on the course before. Appearances were important. Thus, I lived in a 4000 square foot McMansion. Normally this didn't bother me; it was a necessary evil. Tonight, something niggled.

Was it because of my faulty precognitions? Maybe that had me more off-kilter than I thought.

The coldness and impersonality of the muted grays and gleaming metal interior of my house bothered me tonight too. I hurried through the entryway from the garage, ignoring the soaring 30-foot ceilings and open floorplan, eager to get to my bedroom. My heels click-clacked on the marble floors, quieting when I started up the carpeted stairway.

I peeled off my red power-suit, more of an 80s look, I supposed, but still striking.

What should be my next steps? I always had a plan. And Plans B, C, and D, to be honest. I was always prepared and ready with a backup. That was how I attained and maintained my position for so many years.

I'd never had a problem with my precognition before. That niggling sensation returned. Could it be that my precognition wasn't on the fritz? Could it be I'd been misinterpreting? I stood frozen in my walk-in closet as the enormity of that question hit. No, that couldn't be it.

Mist swirled before me and I sat on the carpet to accept the incoming premonition. A person appeared in the haze. A man, I thought. The vision moved closer; yes, it was the back of a man. Dark hair. Black or brown, I wasn't sure. The image stilled and emotions threatened to overwhelm me. Love, hate, power, and betrayal.

"Show me his face," I demanded of the premonition. "Give me more to go on," I insisted. Premonitions didn't work like that and the image stubbornly refused to move. It continued to show the back of this unknown man with dark hair.

Then my premonition did move, though my excitement was short-lived. Instead of showing me something useful about the man, the image shifted to show a female I knew.

Her bright blue eyes flashed in a pale face surrounded by waves of blue hair. The importance of her struck like a physical assault. The image faded and I lay back on the carpet. I stared at the ceiling and considered what I'd received.

I hadn't been given enough to guess the identity of the man in the vision. The second image gave more information. Olivia Williams.

This wasn't the first time this supernatural being had appeared in one of my premonitions. I had dealt with the Paranormal Talent Agency last year when Evie's idiot vampire sire surfaced in Vegas, as a Family Cleaner, no less. He'd been hired to clean Olivia, but luckily, he'd screwed up. She'd already gone underground in New Mexico, if I remembered correctly. My premonition then had been very clear – she needed to remain alive. She was important.

And, now here she was again. Though I wasn't any closer to figuring out her importance. I groaned and returned to the first, more perplexing, image.

A man. With brown or black hair. Eliciting love, hate, power, and betrayal. Irritation spiked through me and I clenched my fists.

With a groan, I relaxed my fists, sat up, and contemplated further.

Who did I know with dark hair? An image of Mark Mammon popped up, smirk in place. Hmm. Hate would not be unexpected connected to him. Power, certainly, as a competitor. Even possibly betrayal, if he was the one who killed the other candidates.

But love? That made no sense that I could understand.

I'd let the premonition percolate a bit and wait to see what information I could glean from the detective tomorrow.

CHAPTER SIX

Jacob Dawson sat opposite me in my office, blue eyes indecipherable. He held a small notebook in one hand and a disposable pen in the other. Ready to take down the pearls of wisdom I'd soon be offering. I bit back a chortle. He leaned forward, maroon button-down dress shirt straining against his shoulders.

"Please, Detective, ask your questions. I have nothing to hide," I volunteered, and his eyebrows rose in surprise.

"Thank you, Councilwoman—"

"Please, call me Barbara," I interrupted, a smile splitting my face. He shuddered and I remembered that my teeth weren't aging well in this body; apparently, they were small and sharp-looking. I brought it down a notch, smiling without showing teeth. Jacob relaxed.

"Barbara," he complied. "Thank you for agreeing to answer my questions."

"Of course, anything to help the investigation."

"Let's start with your decision not to take the bus to the debate."

"That was a last-minute decision," I began, the explanation already sounding rehearsed. The drawback to having repeated the story so many times to members of the press the previous night. He scribbled, mouth pulled down in a frown, while I unspooled the story of needing extra time at campaign headquarters before the debate. I rather magnanimously had not wanted to delay the entire show by holding up the bus until I was ready.

"Do you know why Mark Mammon didn't take the bus either?"

"I do not."

"Have you spoken with Mr. Mammon since the accident?"

"I have not."

"Let me rephrase. Have you been in contact with Mr. Mammon at all since the accident?"

Now it was my turn with the eyebrow raise. "You've already spoken with Mr. Mammon."

"This morning," Jacob confirmed.

"I apologize for the inaccuracy. While it is true I did not speak with him, we exchanged several texts."

"May I see those texts?"

I hesitated for only a moment, but Jacob didn't miss the hesitation. His expression hardened. He expected me to lie.

I smoothed out my own expression. "Of course." My cellphone sat on the desk before me. I unlocked the screen, clicked on the text icon, and slid the phone toward the detective. "The exchange is at the top."

Jacob scrolled through the minimal texts, seeming satisfied. While the texts were terse, and somewhat odd perhaps, there was nothing there suggesting my involvement. Or Mark's, I realized.

"Are you at liberty to tell me what happened?" I asked.

"Normally I wouldn't, but I understand you have sources."

I smirked. He knew I could pick up the phone the instant he turned in any kind of a report and have the full information. I only asked to save myself the hassle.

"The accident was no accident," he said slowly, watching for my reaction.

"What makes you believe that?"

"There was no evidence the driver tried to brake."

"He could have fallen asleep," I offered an alternative explanation.

"He could have. Except a last text came from one of the occupants, stating concern about the driver."

"Anything specific?"

"Nope."

"Wouldn't that suggest the driver did it on purpose?"

"It would."

"Any background on the driver to suggest a motive?"

"Nope."

"The press suggested it might be a terrorist attack."

Jacob frowned. "The press would do well not to speculate at the drop of a hat."

I laughed, knowing there was no love lost between Elizabeth Addison and his girlfriend, Mia. "So probably not terrorism?"

"There's no evidence to suggest that."

"Then why would he do it?"

"We're still investigating, ma'am," Jacob said.

"Could he have done it on behalf of someone else?"

"That's my prevailing theory," he admitted. "Someone who *did* have a reason to kill the candidates."

I chewed on my lower lip. "Any suspects?"

Jacob gave me a blank look and I blanched.

"I'm a suspect."

"I can neither confirm nor deny—"

"And, I presume Mr. Mammon is a suspect."

"I can neither—"

I held up a hand to stop him. "I know, you can neither confirm nor deny my presumption." I tapped my fingernails on the desk. Jacob's eyes cut to them and he watched the fire-engine-red nails tap, tap, tap. My fingernails stilled and he met my gaze.

"I know you don't like me," I began. Jacob had a good poker face. "I also know you know I am… paranormal." Still no reaction. "Understand that I expect you to do your job." He narrowed his eyes at my tone. "I expect you to find out who the actual killer is; prove it isn't me."

Jacob chuckled. "Ma'am, with all due respect, you only got half of that right. I will do my job and find the killer. If you aren't the killer," he gave a fierce smile, "then you have nothing to worry about."

I nodded. "That sounds fair."

His eyes narrowed in disbelief.

"I can be fair. Sometimes a reputation is just a reputation," I reminded him.

"That's true."

"Have I answered all of your questions?"

"Yes, ma'am. I'll be in touch if any follow up is necessary." He stood and I did not.

I inclined my head in response and he stepped from the room. Once he closed my office door, I rose from the desk and stood at the window, overlooking Main Street.

I was clearly a prime suspect. Was that because I hadn't been on the bus? I supposed that was a big factor, given that Mark Mammon was also a suspect.

But, I figured I was more of a suspect than Mark. Not because I had more of a reason to want to eliminate the competition; if that were the sole factor, Mark would have that honor.

No, I knew I was the prime suspect based on my history with Detective Dawson and the Paranormal Talent Agency. So previously I mis-stepped and hired a contract killer to eliminate a witch. I hadn't been successful. Couldn't a demon catch a break?

CHAPTER SEVEN

"Well, this is a surprise," I told the lanky man standing in my doorway. He didn't buy my forced casual tone. Liam Collins, angel and my ex-boyfriend from many, many years ago, somehow was at my house in Las Vegas. Would wonders never cease.

Liam squinted his Caribbean blue eyes and tilted his head. "You look… different."

"Old."

"Mature."

"Old," I insisted, but with a laugh.

"Why?"

I shrugged. "I arrived in Vegas twenty years ago at 25; I needed to age accordingly."

Liam nodded, eyes twinkling. "You still look good."

"For an old lady."

"For an any-age woman."

My cheeks flushed. Dang, that man could still get me, even after hundreds of years. He ran a hand through his curly brown hair, still a touch too long and unruly, and gave me a crooked smile.

"May I come in?"

I stepped aside to allow him access, enjoying the view from behind as much as from the front. But this was a no-win rabbit hole for me. I made my choice a long time ago. Liam paused just inside the door, waiting for me to lead the way. He followed me to the black leather couches in the living room. I didn't miss the frown flit across his face. Guess he didn't like the décor.

"To what do I owe the honor of your visit? I had a long day at work and I'm tired."

Liam allowed a bittersweet smile before getting down to business. "I would like to request your assistance."

"So formal."

"It seems appropriate, now."

"Because I'm the head of the supernatural underworld for the Vegas region?"

"Something like that."

"What can I assist you with?"

"Mark Mammon ordered the hit on the mayoral candidates."

I raised a single eyebrow. "That's a bold accusation." Not that I disagreed.

"You were supposed to be on that bus."

Anger surged through me at this apparent confirmation. "Was I?"

Liam laughed, the loud sound echoing through my cavernous space. "You're kidding, right? The Barbara I knew would never have doubted it."

A small sigh escaped. "You're right. I knew. To hear it confirmed…"

Liam reached out to touch a lock of my brown hair, recently set free from my typical bun I wore for work. "I'm glad you weren't on the bus."

I jerked back and he dropped his hand. "Thank you. Though you know it wouldn't have hurt me."

"Still."

An uncomfortable warmth spread through me. "Does Mark know I'm a demon?" I changed the subject.

"We don't know."

"He would know a bus crash couldn't kill me," I continued, more to myself. "Anyway, what can I do for you?"

"I'd like to request your help in us proving his guilt, so he can be held accountable."

"Us?"

He smirked. "You know them. A group connected with… I believe its nickname is the Paranormal Talent Agency."

My eyes rolled in reflex at the phrase and Liam chuckled.

"I guess you do know them."

"How do *you* know them?"

"I was told to reach out to Mia, and she introduced me to Catherine."

Catherine Rodham, head of the Paranormal Talent Agency in Las Vegas. Mia Fynn, film producer and 200-year-old nixie. And, Jacob, Mia's boyfriend, had already interviewed me. I wondered when Evie Jones, the snarky vampire actress, would pop up too. Were we getting the whole band back together? I snorted. "What's the plan?" The image of the dark-haired man from my vision surfaced. Could it have been Liam, not Mark?

Liam tilted his head again. "What just went through your mind?"

I hesitated. Oh heck, why not? He already knew about my precognitive powers. "I had a premonition about a dark-haired man involving power and betrayal." And love, my mind reminded me. I smacked that thought down.

Liam nodded. "That could definitely be Mark. He's certainly power-hungry and wouldn't hesitate to betray you."

"He already tried to kill me," I responded drily.

"Too true."

"Here's the thing. If I'm being completely honest—" His eyebrows rose a fraction and I flushed. "—my involvement in the past has not gone well with the Agency."

"I heard they cost you a minion."

"Nice, Liam, very nice." He chuckled and I grinned. This felt so easy, like before— My grin dropped. "My plan had been to stay out of it. The vision was quite indistinct." And I don't want to make a mistake, my mind added. I grimaced.

"That doesn't sound like the Barbara I know, either. You want to stay on the sidelines, licking your wounds?" The taunt was gentle, but still I bristled. His reverse psychology was totally going to work.

"Fine, I'll help."

"Fantastic," he replied with a broad smile.

"Did you win the bet?"

"Bet?"

"I know you. Since gambling with river rocks as a boy, you always liked wagering."

He winked.

"Did you win the bet with, I'm guessing Catherine, on whether or not I'd agree to help?"

His smile widened. "Maybe."

I laughed, and suddenly was very aware of the heat between us. Just like old times; 100 years together left an impression. Our smiles fell at the same time and his blue eyes gazed into my black ones. He broke the contact first, rising to his feet and heading toward the front door.

"I'll let the crew know and we'll make plans to meet," he called over his shoulder.

I stood slower and followed him to the door, where he paused and faced me.

"I'm sorry for the circumstances, Barbara, but I'm glad to see you."

I nodded stiffly. "Thank you."

Liam's smile wavered at my failure to echo his sentiment. "I'll get your number from Catherine and let you know when we're meeting tomorrow. Is there any time that doesn't work for you?"

I shook my head. Mute.

He took my hand in his, warmth suffusing me. "Until tomorrow." He released my hand and closed the door.

I walked back to the couch and collapsed on the supple surface. Working with the Paranormal Talent Agency crew could be a good thing. It would keep me in the loop. And they might even have some good ideas, I grudgingly admitted.

My involvement had nothing to do with Liam, with the way he looked at me, how my body responded when he touched my hair, my hand. Nope, not at all.

Then why was I counting down the hours until I saw him again?

CHAPTER EIGHT

Production staff called out uncomfortable greetings as I strode past them. I managed not to roll my eyes. Sycophants. None of them liked me, they just feared me. Like I'd care if they didn't say hello. Okay, maybe I'd care. Luckily, my unhelpful thoughts short-circuited when I spotted the group with whom I was meeting.

Liam had texted the address this morning – an independent film location in Sun City. A simple three-bedroom, one-story home in the 55+ community within Summerlin. Since most of the group was in the entertainment world, and my image involved keeping my finger on the pulse of that industry, nobody would question my presence. Even if they weren't thrilled by it.

Chatter ceased the moment I stood in the doorway of a back bedroom. An eight-foot, white, plastic folding table sat in the middle of the space. A group of actors and crew, a mix of human and supernatural, occupied the metal folding chairs surrounding the table.

Liam jumped to his feet and hurried to me. "Barbara, welcome. We're glad you're here."

"Not all of us," a voice muttered and Evie Jones smirked when our eyes met. The 1920s blond vampire actress was easily the snarkiest of the bunch.

"Evie, that's enough," Catherine Rodham, head of the Paranormal Talent Agency, chastised her, but with a smile in her blue eyes.

Liam led me to an empty chair between him and Catherine. I lowered into the uncomfortable seat and gazed around the table. In addition to Liam, Catherine, and Evie, four others were present. Including Robin, my ex-minion (also a witch and owner of another talent agency) and her new boyfriend, Jackson, the witch who I tried unsuccessfully to have killed a few months ago. Guess they were willing to let bygones be bygones. I honed in on one of the humans present.

"Jacob, I didn't know you involved civilians in your cases."

"Ma'am, even you must admit they've demonstrated their helpfulness before," he responded, his eyes meeting his girlfriend's. Mia blushed.

"Touché. What's the plan?" I wanted to get down to business so I could leave. The tension radiating off the group around me was suffocating. I imagined Catherine was struggling with the emotions too, given her empath abilities; although I wasn't sure she understood the extent of them yet any more than I did.

"I've caught everyone up. Our goal is to stop Mark Mammon," Liam began, blue eyes sparking, "before anyone else gets hurt." Everyone murmured their agreement. "Thoughts on how to do that?"

"Can't we just hire someone to kill him?" I asked, as a joke. Nobody laughed. Tough crowd. "I'm kidding," I assured them.

"It's a bit too soon for that," Robin bit off.

Maybe we weren't letting bygones be bygones. I stayed quiet.

"We need to, at a minimum, incapacitate him," Liam said, "but, like it or not, we may need to eliminate him."

"That doesn't seem necessary," Catherine objected.

"I hate to agree with the demon," Evie chimed in, "except that she and Liam are probably right. Mark's a demon—" Her eyes cut to mine. "—and we know how difficult they can be."

"Hey, I've never actually killed anyone," I protested.

"Not for lack of trying," Jackson tossed off.

"I'm sorry that I tried to kill you," I told him formally. "It seemed the most expedient at the time. I was mistaken." I thought I was mistaken, anyway; I failed, certainly.

"Thank you," he accepted hesitantly. "I guess."

"Evie and Liam are right," Mia said, and several people gasped. I supposed she was usually peacemaker. I knew her kind could use their voices to calm beings down; and bewitch people, but I doubted that was the reason for the gasps.

"You can't mean that," Catherine argued.

Mia ran her hand through her green hair and shrugged. "He's a demon bent on removing threat and consolidating power." She deliberately avoided eye contact with me. This wasn't awkward at all. Not one bit. She continued. "Unlike some—" She threw me a bone. "—I don't think he'd be amenable to backing off."

"We don't know that," Catherine said.

"Besides, folks, planning to kill someone is a crime," Jacob the homicide detective reminded the table. "Let's be clear on this. Our goal is to stop him, not kill him. If he dies in the process, that's different."

"Since Mark texted Barbara before the crash, it would make sense that she would be our liaison to him, so to speak," Evie said. Nods of agreement met her statement.

"We need to get him to admit to causing the crash," Jacob added.

"Or hiring someone to do it," Robin amended, with a side glance at me.

I sighed.

"Will you want her to wear a wire?" Liam asked. Did I hear an undertone of concern?

Jacob shook his head. "Given how you supernatural folks are—" Mia gave him a playful smack on the arm and he smiled. "It's probably better if at least some of us are present, including me. That way, she just needs to get him to admit he did it. Then I can arrest him."

"Sounds so simple when you put it that way," Evie said drily and I laughed. Heads swiveled toward me.

"He's a demon. We don't know his power. It could be passive or active," I reminded them.

Jacob frowned. "What's the likelihood it's active?"

I shrugged. "If he caused the accident himself, then I'd say it's pretty active. If he hired someone, he probably has a passive power. I don't know."

"That's not very helpful, Barbara," Evie taunted.

"Watch the glowing, ma'am," Jacob warned and I realized my eyes were burning red.

"Regardless of his power type, our goal is to get him to admit he caused or ordered the accident. If his power type turns out to be active, you guys can do your thing," I waved my hand dismissively.

"Our *thing* saved Jackson and thwarted your plans," Robin spat out.

"Thwarted?" I snorted. I took an emotional step back. "Look, I get that none of you like me." Except maybe Liam. I hoped. "I appreciate your willingness to help me." And I was a bit surprised to discover that was true. It had been a long time since I felt connected to anyone, even superficially. "We have five days until the election. Five days to stop him. Since I'm in his crosshairs, I'll be our liaison, bait, whatever you want to call it."

"This is starting to be a habit with us," Catherine said with a shake of her head.

"Let's plan on two meetings with Mark," Liam said. "The first one, to explore and build rapport, and the second one, to get an admission of guilt and lower the boom."

Nods of agreement again.

"We'll start tonight." He met my gaze. "I'll stay with Barbara for this one."

A flush crept up my neck and I wondered if the others could see it. "That's acceptable," I agreed, and Liam grinned.

"This is quite a vehicle," Liam commented as he hoisted himself into the Escalade. I ignored the veiled barb and started the engine. It purred in response. The drive from Sun City to my gated community took about thirty minutes; thankfully construction on Summerlin Parkway was finally completed. At least for now.

Liam stared out the window into the dark for the entirety of the drive. I tapped my fingers on the leather steering wheel in time to the 1980s music on the radio. Yeah, I liked my 80s rock.

"Keep it simple," Liam finally spoke once we were seated on the couch.

I raised a single eyebrow.

"I know you know what you're doing," he clarified. "But, you know, when you send the text, keep it simple." He smiled, dimples forming on his cheeks, and I laughed.

"Got it, boss." I found Mark's previous text and started typing.

We need to meet.

We do?

Yes. Tonight.

Where?

My house.

Be there in thirty.

"He knows where you live?" Liam's tone betrayed his concern and irritation.

"He's never been here before. It's public record."

"Hmm, okay."

"What do we do while we wait?"

An unreadable look crossed Liam's face before he responded. "Let's review our game plan."

"When Mark arrives, I'm going to ask him his plan. I'm not going to ask him if he killed the candidates."

"Succinct."

"I try."

We shared a smile.

"I've missed this," I blurted out. Liam and I wore matching looks of surprise before he responded with a ghost of a smile.

"If you could go back, would you make the same choice?" Liam stared intently, waiting for my answer.

I hesitated. Go back 400 years? Our flirtation was always fun, but it wasn't my destiny. "Probably," I admitted and he nodded.

"Have you thought about how you'll ask him?" Liam deftly changed the subject.

"So it doesn't sound like a trap?"

"Something like that."

"I'll just play on his expectations."

"Yeah?"

"If he knows I'm a demon, he wouldn't have expected me to die. He has to figure I'll want to know more. He almost certainly expected me to call a meeting like this."

"At your home?" Liam pursed his lips.

"Less threatening that way. More open."

"Maybe."

"Probably." I shrugged. "He and I have been playing this game a long time."

"Indeed."

That unreadable look passed over Liam's face again. The doorbell rang.

"He's here," I said needlessly.

"I'll hide in the bedroom."

I bit my lip at the image. Liam smiled wolfishly before loping out of the room. I crossed to the front door in seconds, took a deep breath, and opened it with authority.

CHAPTER NINE

Mark Mammon was a handsome man, and knew it. He sidled close to me in the open doorway and offered a sly smile.

"May I come in?"

Taken aback, I hesitated in responding.

"You asked me here, remember?" He winked.

I shook my head. "Of course, come in." I stood to the side and he sauntered past. Hand on my hip, I watched with increasing irritation as he made himself right at home on the living room couch. He crossed one slacks-clad leg over the other.

"Are you coming?"

"Mmm-mm," I mumbled and followed his path.

Heat rolled off of him. I inched back further from him on the couch. His knowing smile snapped me out of it. I was a demon, too. Why was I letting him get to me?

"Thank you for meeting with me," I started. "You must be wondering why I invited you here."

Mark's black eyes stayed on my face, unblinking. Two could play that game. I allowed a bit of red to glow around my pupils. His smile slipped a fraction, but there was no exclamation of surprise. That answered the question of whether or not he knew I was a demon.

"On the night of the bus crash, you texted me. Why?"

"Why wouldn't I?" His look of confusion was convincing. If I didn't know better, I'd believe it.

"You expected me to be on the bus," I pushed.

"We were both supposed to be on the bus."

"Why weren't you on the bus?"

"Last minute change of plans."

"That was convenient."

"For you, too."

"Did you know the driver never hit the brakes?"

A slight rise of his eyebrows was the only indicator that my question surprised him. "How do you know that?"

"Sources. You didn't answer my question."

"I didn't."

That stymied me for a moment. "What changed in your plans to keep you off the bus?"

"What changed in yours?"

I thinned my lips in displeasure.

Mark laughed. "I can do this all night." He leaned his elbows on his knees. "Why do you care about the crash?"

"Why should I care if someone tried to kill me?"

He shrugged. "They didn't succeed."

"No. It's almost as if they didn't know I was a demon and couldn't be killed that way."

Mark rolled with my admission. "Or they had some other intent."

I lifted an eyebrow.

"Maybe the goal wasn't to kill all the candidates. You've been around. You know what the reduction in candidates means. It's easier now. It's just between you and me," he said with a grin. "With only two candidates, one of us will have the majority in the primary election in five days, and then there won't be a need for a general election later in the year."

"Technically, the other names remain on the ballot, this close to the election. People can still vote for any of us, even the dead ones."

He frowned and I smiled.

"You've been around so long and you didn't know that?"

He coughed and my smile widened.

"Besides, possibly someone may still try to kill me. Or you," I added, watching for even the most minute of reactions.

"That's true. Anything could happen."

"You wouldn't happen to know more about it, would you?"

Mark coyly smiled. "What more could I know?"

"Nothing, I guess." I bit my lower lip, an action he didn't miss. "How did you do it?" I finally just baldly asked him.

"Hypothetically?"

"If you wish."

"How would I do it?"

"Yes."

"Wouldn't you like to know."

I stood. "I think we're done here." This was one of those times I wished for my enchanted bullets. Immortal demons could be killed; you just needed the right weapon. He infuriated me.

He rose and smoothed imaginary wrinkles from the front of his navy-blue cashmere sweater. "Thank you for the invitation. This has been… educational."

"Indeed." I walked toward the front door, listening to the sound of his footsteps behind me on the marble.

At the doorway, Mark took my hand and kissed it. "Until next time." I snatched it back, ignoring his grin, and flashed red eyes. "Now, now, Barbara. That's not necessary."

I watched him until he got in his car, then I closed the door. I didn't slam it, though I really, really wanted to. When I turned around, Liam was standing next to the couch, that unreadable look on his face.

CHAPTER TEN

"That went well," I spat out, stalking over to stand beside Liam. His face softened. He took my hands in his, startling me.

"It wasn't that bad. We learned more information."

"Like he doesn't know how local elections work?"

Liam laughed and released my hands. We sat on the couch, knees inches apart. "Yeah, we did learn that," he agreed.

I rolled my head in a circle, releasing tension from my neck. "I don't know why I let him infuriate me. I'm a demon who's been in power here for years." That unreadable look passed again on Liam's face. I considered commenting this time, but it vanished almost as fast as it arrived.

"I understand you're… dissatisfied with how that meeting went."

"That's an understatement."

"No doubt. I think, though, we should focus on what else we learned."

"Ah, that angel positivity," I quipped and Liam chuckled.

"You had that once, too," he reminded me.

I sobered. "That was a long time ago. But, you're right. Although he didn't acknowledge it, I think we're safe in assuming our presumption was correct, given his *hypothetical.*"

"An assumption about our presumption? Say that three times fast," he joked.

A giggle escaped before I could demand he take this seriously. "I don't think I can," I said instead. "You know what I mean!"

"I do," he said softly. The energy between us thickened. I wondered if he could see my desire in my black eyes as clearly as I could see his desire in his blue ones. He blinked and glanced away, breaking the moment. Disappointment flooded me.

Back to business. "We confirmed indirectly he's the killer – or at least arranged the killing. He also suggested I'm still on his hit list. Not that he'd be successful," I boasted.

"You're that confident?"

"When you have a built-in warning system…"

"Of course."

No need to mention I wasn't sure if my precognition was on the fritz. I'd stick with being confident; it was my area of strength, after all.

"I trust you're not suggesting we not worry about him."

"Absolutely not. He's a danger. Possibly to me physically. And politically." Liam and I wore matching frowns. I suspected his frown had a different meaning. No reason to speculate on that now.

"Plus, he could hurt other innocents," Liam reminded me.

"Right, right. Our goal remains unchanged," I concluded.

"I'll speak with Catherine, Mia, and the others. Catch them up on tonight's meeting. Our goal is still to get him to confess. I'll speak with them about how best to approach that, since tonight you basically asked him, and he refused to answer."

"I think we've shown the direct approach won't work. We need to sneak up on him, verbally."

"I'll let you know what they say."

"Thanks. And thanks for being here tonight."

"Of course." Liam offered a crooked smile.

Impulsively, I leaned in to give Liam a hug. He tensed and I began to pull away, then his strong arms encircled me. He felt good. This felt good. An angel and a demon wouldn't have a future together – I had made sure of that years ago – but that didn't mean I couldn't enjoy this time.

"I have to go," he whispered into my ear, his breath warm against my skin.

I pulled back and offered him my own crooked smile. "I know."

"I'll let myself out."

I nodded, not trusting myself to speak. Liam rested his hand against my cheek for a moment before standing. He walked toward the front door, his shoes silent against the marble. I continued staring at the door after he was gone, until the swirling mist informed me of an impending premonition.

CHAPTER ELEVEN

I reclined on the couch, hoping this premonition would clarify what I had seen before. A man appeared in the haze. I frowned. It was the same man as before, still only visible from behind. Dark hair. Feelings of love, hate, power, and betrayal. A frustrated growl slipped out. This wasn't helping. I didn't need a repeat of the prior premonition.

As if hearing my unspoken gripe, the vision faded and a new one appeared. I sighed. Olivia Williams again, blue eyes sparkling, a half-smile on her face. Blue hair contained in a French braid. The smile dropped and Olivia stared, seemingly at me, beseeching me.

To do what?

Olivia turned and walked away. After about ten feet, she stopped. My breath caught in my throat. This was different from last time. She glared at me over her shoulder. When I didn't seem to "get it", she shook her head and gestured that I should follow her. My vision of the image zoomed in and she smiled – before blinking out of existence.

The dark-haired man replaced her. I squished my eyes closed tighter, willing the man to turn around so I could see his face. The mist obscured even the texture of his hair. His head dipped back. In pain? In joy? The image vanished and my eyes popped open.

I realized with a start that I was drenched in sweat. This was an unwelcome development. A frown flitted across my face as I considered this new premonition. The dark-haired man, I still assumed, must be Mark or Liam. I bit my lip in concentration. Maybe I could be more certain if I figured out the emphasis on Olivia. Because the premonition definitely emphasized her.

Olivia's apparent irritation; I assumed that was with me. But why? She beckoned me toward her. Again, the question of why reverberated in my brain. She had been important to my visions before, and here she was yet again. If my precognition was back on track, it was even more important for me to correctly figure out its intention with these images.

Olivia beckoned me. That much was clear. And it was related to the dark-haired man. Given those overriding emotions, especially of hate and betrayal, I felt safe in believing the dark-haired man was Mark Mammon.

What would Olivia have to do with Mark? Like a lightning bolt, if that wasn't too cliché, it hit me. Olivia came to my premonition before when she was being targeted by a hitman. She wanted me to reach out to her… for assistance in removing the source of the hate and betrayal? I ruminated on this possibility.

What if?

I organized my thoughts.

What if the premonition was telling me that Olivia could solve the problem with Mark? I didn't fully know her background. My previous premonition featuring her had never clearly stated her importance. I'd just trusted that she was important.

But I'd heard rumors that Olivia had taken care of supernatural beings in the past. Could she be a contract killer like Evie's sire had been?

I sat up and snapped my fingers. That had to be it. The premonition was telling me to hire Olivia to kill Mark.

A voice at the back of my mind reminded me I had never killed anyone before and that maybe now wasn't the time to start. I stomped on that little voice.

If my visions were accurate again, I didn't want to disregard one. Just because it had gone sideways before didn't mean this was the wrong choice.

With another shake of my head, I walked to my home office to fire up my laptop. The last I heard, Olivia was in New Mexico.

I dashed off a quick email to a contact there requesting information.

That voice in my head reminded me of the disastrous last time I tried to hire a contract killer. My fists clenched on the desk. This time would be different.

A ding announced a new email and I scanned it quickly. My contacts were good. I called the number listed.

CHAPTER TWELVE

"Thank you for agreeing to see me on such short notice," I greeted the blue-haired ethereal woman now seated on my couch. I didn't normally like to conduct business in my home, but that seemed to be the way this situation was staying. A nervous energy trilled through me. Something about this woman… being. I wasn't entirely sure what she was. She wasn't human, I could tell that.

"Thank you for sending the private jet for me," Olivia Williams responded, an odd glint in her bright blue eyes. "I've never traveled on one before. It was an interesting experience."

"It seemed the most efficient. I'm glad you enjoyed it." I paused, taking in her flowing white shift, and regal bearing. She looked like an angel, if I was being honest. A knot formed in my stomach. Was I about to make another huge mistake?

No, I had to trust my instincts. How much to tell her? She stared at me impassively, waiting while I wrestled with my inner thoughts. So serene. Screw it.

"In four days, a primary election for the mayor of Las Vegas will be held. A fatal bus crash reduced the field to myself and one other candidate, Mark Mammon." Her eyes narrowed for a moment at the name. "Do you know him?"

"I do."

Distracted from my purpose, I switched directions. "What can you tell me about him?"

"What do you already know?"

"He's a demon older than I am."

Olivia nodded. "Indeed."

"That's all I really know. I could give you the details of the names my investigator ran down, if you'd like. All it does is confirm those basics. He's a demon older than I am," I repeated.

"Mark… Mammon," she stumbled at his last name, "was friends with Caesar."

I gasped. That made him Roman, as I'd suspected. Also, over 2000 years old.

She held up her hand. "That's all I can tell you."

Interesting that she didn't say that was all she knew. I returned to my original goal. "I understand that you take care of problems."

Olivia gave a Cheshire-cat grin. "That's one way to describe what I do."

Her response threw me. "How would you describe what you do?"

"I reward and punish behavior."

Hmm, okay. "That's an interesting description," I said cautiously, mind swirling. Maybe my sources were wrong?

"What is it you would like me to do?"

I seized on her earlier words. "I would like you to punish someone for his behavior."

She nodded. "Mark Mammon, I presume. For what?"

"For killing the other mayoral candidates."

She tilted her head. "You have proof of this?"

I reddened. "It's fairly well acknowledged."

"It is."

I couldn't tell if this was agreement or simply confirming what I had said. I felt flustered. "I'm also worried that he may still try to kill me," I added. "He implied as much to me." She nodded again. "There's only four days until the election…" I continued before trailing off.

"You would need this situation handled before that deadline."

Once again, I couldn't tell if this was agreement or simply confirming she understood what I had said.

"Your eyes are glowing," she said.

The conversational tone calmed me. "Apologies."

She waved off the apology. "The situation will be handled before the deadline."

"Um, great?"

"I'll be in touch." She grinned again and stood from the couch. "I'll see myself out."

When the door closed behind her, I released the breath I hadn't realized I was holding. I had done it. Mark Mammon would be a problem no more. And then I could get back to managing this city and the paranormal underworld.

CHAPTER THIRTEEN

Butterflies fluttered in my belly and I nearly rolled my eyes at myself. Nervous like a teenage girl before a first date. When Liam texted to invite me to lunch, I didn't even try to deny the thrill that went through me. It dimmed a little at the location choice – *Soprannaturale*, a paranormals-only café near my office. To say a demon would not be welcome there would be an understatement. But maybe Liam didn't know that.

"Are you in the right place, ma'am?" The owner, Antonio DiMaio, greeted me formally and with a strained smile. I glanced over his shoulder to find Liam. He lifted a hand when our eyes met and I gestured toward him.

"Yes, I'm meeting someone," I answered, pointing toward Liam.

Antonio shifted to look behind him and his brown eyes took in Liam. The owner stepped to the side. "Welcome."

It was my first time in the café. Standard wannabe Italian-café style, frankly. Still seemed like an odd choice for Liam. A genuine smile formed though as I began the long walk through the café. Until I passed a large occupied table (were those elves?) and spotted the secluded booth Liam had chosen. A confused frown replaced my smile. Liam was not alone. Catherine, Mia, Robin, Jackson, and Jacob were seated around him. And Olivia. What the—

I plastered a fake smile on my face. "This is a surprise."

"Please sit, Councilwoman," Jacob requested.

I complied, sliding in next to Liam. Tension rolled off of him, mitigating any joy I might have felt in sitting so close. "Councilwoman? I see we're back with formalities," I joked.

"It has come to my attention that you allegedly committed criminal solicitation," Jacob responded.

My gaze involuntarily swung to Olivia, whose face remained impassive, assessing. "Is that so?"

"Don't disrespect us by denying it, Barbara." The corners of Liam's mouth turned down and genuine sadness shown in his eyes.

Guilt flared and I tamped it down. "This is an ambush," I accused him.

"That's one way to look at it," he responded.

"How else should I look at it?"

"An intervention," Mia answered for him, her soothing voice rolling over me.

"Stop trying to calm me," I commanded, feeling my eyes burn. Mia nodded but did not deny the implied accusation. The feeling of calm receded. "An intervention?" The word choice hit me. "Are you helping me choose the right path?" I barked a nasty laugh and aimed a mocking grin at Robin, who flushed. She and I had had a similar conversation recently. Something about how I could choose the path of the righteous. Or some such nonsense.

"You always have choices," Jackson added, with a loaded look at Olivia.

I frowned, perplexed by the missed meaning in that glance.

"Why did you hire Olivia to kill Mark?" Liam asked, a tone of desperation in his voice that further baffled me.

I debated whether or not to admit I committed the… what did Jacob call it? Criminal solicitation.

As if hearing my internal debate, Jacob drily commented, "As an officer of the court, I am ceding our interest in this possible case to the underworld to handle as it sees fit."

"So you can tell the truth," Catherine explained.

I stared around the booth at these people, these beings, trying to understand why any of them cared about this. We weren't friends. Were they just looking for a way to trip me up? My gaze ended on Liam and the hurt there unexpectedly stung.

Why would he be surprised? The memory of our final argument flashed through my mind. After 100 years together, I had grown weary of humanity's stupidity and wanted to do things my way. Liam tried to argue that I was going through a rough patch and things would be fine. But, no. I yelled at him that being an angel was too limiting and I'd rather put my self-interest first. His eyes almost comically widened, his mouth dropped open. A blinding light bathed me, warmth that became sharp like needles across my entire body. The last I heard was Liam crying out my name while I screamed. I awoke in darkness like molasses. Then, I blanked again, waking a final time as a demon. It was glorious. Not answering to the angel bureaucracy. Not worrying if my choices hurt anybody else. Even the pain of losing Liam faded over time to a dull ache. I'd thought I'd gotten over him entirely, until he appeared at my door.

In any event, my hiring Olivia simply reinforced the decision I made all that time ago to follow my own path. I lifted a single shoulder in a blasé shrug. "Sure, why not? I hired Olivia. Well, I suppose to be accurate, I thought I hired Olivia. To kill Mark Mammon," I clearly enunciated.

"I thought we agreed to a plan," Liam protested.

I shrugged again. "I decided to go in another direction."

"Why?" His disappointed eyes searched mine, as if he thought he'd find some answer in their black fathomless depths. Hardly.

"Expediency." My clipped tone brooked no argument and nobody tried. I stood. "Thank you for the invitation to discuss this issue," I stated with a nod at the group. "I obviously did not hire Olivia as I thought I had. And now that I'm on your radar," I directed toward Jacob, "I will not attempt to hire anyone else. I appreciate your concern for my handling of the situation, I offer my sincerest apologies for any inconvenience, and I will handle my issues on my own."

With nary a glance at the table – and especially not Liam – I spun in my sensible shoes and strode from the café. I kept my head held high and avoided eye contact.

The café door closed behind me and I walked to my SUV, the cool spring air nipping at the exposed skin on my face. I considered what had happened. A crushing sense of defeat enveloped me.

Either my precognition was still broken, or I massively misunderstood its meaning. Olivia had some importance I just wasn't getting. And I probably blew any chance I had with Liam. I slammed the door to my vehicle shut. The engine roared to life.

What chance with Liam? That ship sailed hundreds of years ago.

My resolve hardened. I may have blown it with Liam. And I might not have any idea who or what Olivia was. But I could still beat Mark in the primary election and secure my seat and position of power in the paranormal underworld. I had gotten sidetracked by Liam's reemergence in my life and the strange underpinnings of my evolving relationships with the Paranormal Talent Agency folks. That was done. I'd do this my way.

CHAPTER FOURTEEN

Bright set lights blinded me and then lowered. I smiled at the brunette sitting across from me. Her own smile's wattage dimmed slightly. Yeah, my teeth. What's a demon to do? You made sacrifices to your human form.

"Are you ready?" Elizabeth Addison, host of the morning show, *Entertainment Daily*, and sometimes anchor for the news, recovered her smile.

"Always."

She flicked a glance toward her producer and then nodded at me. She faced the camera closest to her. "Good evening, Las Vegas. Welcome to the news at 6." She worked her way through the promos for that evening's show, before sobering.

"Last week, a fatal bus crash rocked the upcoming mayoral election, leaving only two candidates for the primaries, Barbara Knollman, a current city councilwoman, and Mark Mammon, the dark horse challenger. Here to answer questions in advance of what has turned into the most-watched regional election on the West Coast, is current councilwoman, Barbara Knollman." She turned to face me. "Welcome, Councilwoman."

"Thank you, as always, for having me. Even under such unusual circumstances."

"Unusual? Interesting choice of words."

"In my decades in politics, I'm not sure I've ever heard of, let alone been involved in, an election where several candidates were killed. I think that qualifies as unusual."

Elizabeth laughed a fake, newscaster laugh, then grew serious. "Let's talk about those deaths. I understand that you were interviewed by the police following the crash."

"That is correct. Both myself and Mr. Mammon were interviewed. As the remaining candidates—"

"Who were supposed to be on the bus," Elizabeth interrupted and added as an aside for viewers.

"Yes, who were supposed to be on the bus," I continued smoothly.

"Why weren't you on the bus?" Elizabeth interrupted again with her question.

My eyebrows rose but I smiled. "I've given you that information, remember, Elizabeth? The night of the accident."

She lifted her hands in a mea culpa, and continued. "You told me that night that you had a change in your schedule. What was that change again?" She tilted her head and didn't quite hide her smirk.

"As I told Metro, that is confidential campaign information that I am not at liberty to disclose."

"And Metro bought that?"

"Excuse me?" I barely maintained my conversational tone.

"You're the candidate," she said pointedly. "What reason could there be that you couldn't choose to disclose?"

"Not everything is intended for public consumption, as much as you wish that wasn't the case," I chided her with a fake grin. Time to get back on track. "It was expected that we would be interviewed. Metro did a stellar job, as always."

Elizabeth cocked an eyebrow. "Have they arrested anybody, though?"

"That's complicated, Elizabeth. We don't want them to rush into a wrongful arrest."

"Do they have any suspects? Did they clear the other candidate?" She pushed with her questions.

I thinned my lips, as if in thought. This was the opening I was waiting for. "I've been cleared."

"What about Mark Mammon?"

"To my knowledge, he has not been cleared."

"Are you saying Mark Mammon is responsible for the other candidates' murders?" Elizabeth asked salaciously.

With wide-eyed innocence, I held up my hands. "Of course not. I would never be so incendiary as to accuse someone of something so heinous—"

"But?"

I shrugged. "But he and I were the only ones not on the bus. And the citizens of the Valley have known me for two decades." I looked away from Elizabeth's hazel eyes and directly into the camera. "Who is Mark Mammon?"

"And there you have it folks," Elizabeth said to the viewers. "Not an accusation at all, a concern. Do you share the Councilwoman's concerns? Let us know on social media." The brunette newscaster provided the handles for the station's social media accounts. When the producer signaled the live feed ended, she turned to me with a wide smile. "That was awesome. I'll bet our numbers will skyrocket."

"Glad I could help. Thank you for squeezing me in tonight."

And now for the fallout. In three, two, one…

CHAPTER FIFTEEN

"Good evening, Liam. Come on in." I stepped to the side to allow him entry. His blue eyes met my black ones and with a slight shake of his head, he did as I invited.

We sat on the couch in silence for several long moments. Liam stared at me, probably uncertain as to what he wanted to say. I put him out of his misery.

"Liam, what can I do for you?" I smiled to take the edge off of the question.

"I'm worried."

"For me?"

"Of course, for you!"

"I've taken care of myself for literally hundreds of years," I reminded my ex-paramour. "I can manage for the three days until the election."

"Do you not understand you don't poke the beast? He already killed the other candidates!"

"I'm a demon, too. He doesn't scare me."

"He should."

"What do you know that I don't?"

"Nothing, I'm just worried for you." Liam clasped my hands in his, setting off tingles throughout my body in response. He rubbed the tops of my hands with his thumbs.

"Mmm, that feels good," slipped out before I could censor myself.

Liam's eyes dilated in response. We savored the moment before reality crashed back in. "This is what we could have had."

I withdrew my hands. "I know." Had I made the right choice? I'd never second guessed myself as much as I had just in the past few days. I hated it.

"That day when you," he swallowed audibly, "declared you didn't want to be an angel anymore…" Pain shone in his eyes. "I loved you. I thought we'd be together forever."

Stab me in the heart, why don't you? I bit my lower lip. "I loved you too." I shrugged. "Sometimes that's not enough. I made the choice that was right for me." My voice sounded much more confident than I actually felt. When I'd woken up as a demon and realized I'd lost Liam with my choice to reject being an angel… well, let's just say the pain hurt worse than even falling to Hell. But the decision was made, and over the years focusing on myself became even easier. And fun, if I'm honest.

"I'll always care for you."

"You will?"

Hurt glinted in his eyes. "Of course, how could you doubt that?"

"I'm sorry. This has been tough." I was horrified when my voice cracked on the last word. Liam reached a hand toward me and when I didn't pull away, he stroked my cheek with his palm. His skin was rough; I wondered what he'd been doing all these years.

"Please be more careful," he begged me.

"I'm not sure it's in my nature," I said with a laugh, breaking the tension.

"I suppose not." Liam stood and smiled down at me. "I should leave." I stood next to him. "Think about what you really want. Okay?"

"Okay," I promised, but I might as well have had my fingers crossed. I'd chosen this path a long time ago; and I was so close to cementing my control of Las Vegas for both the normal and the paranormal. I wasn't giving that up. Though his being here sure was confounding me. We walked to the front door and I opened it for him to leave. "Goodbye, Liam."

"Until later, Barbara," he responded with a grin.

"Until later," I amended, matching his grin.

I closed the door behind him, stood there listening to his engine start and him backing his car down my driveway. I waited a few more moments, awash with uncertainty.

About to turn away, I paused when I heard tires on the driveway. Had Liam come back?

"I must not be the visitor you were expecting," Mia said, her laughter like tinkling bells.

Guess my poker face was slipping. "What can I do for you, Mia?"

"May I come in?"

"Of course." I repeated my earlier actions and in moments, Mia and I sat next to each other on my couch.

"I'm sure you're wondering why I'm here."

"The thought had crossed my mind."

"I saw your interview earlier this evening."

"What did you think?"

"Seemed risky to deliberately antagonize Mark."

Had she and Liam compared notes? Sheesh. "It's only three more days. I wanted him to know that I'm not cowering, waiting for him to strike." My eyes burned and Mia's expression confirmed I was glowing red. I took a calming breath.

"Why didn't you stick to the plan?"

"Are we going to repeat the conversation from the café? Because that didn't really go well."

Mia appeared thoughtful for a moment. "Barbara, we've had a checkered history."

I chuckled. "That's one way of putting it."

She smiled. "But that doesn't have to determine our future."

"What are you saying?"

"I haven't been around quite as long as you have. And you've been mostly benevolent, if not exactly honest and open."

"I'm a demon," I reminded her, flabbergasted by this continuing insistence I be something I wasn't. Just because a long time ago, I had different priorities. Couldn't people keep track of that? I put myself first.

"You could still work with us and prove Mark guilty. It still ultimately benefits you," she said with a sly look.

"Now that's a better way to entice me," I confirmed flippantly.

Mia smiled but disappointment shone in her eyes. "Olivia—" She abruptly stopped.

"Olivia what?"

Mia shook her head. "She can help with handling Mark."

"Is that all?"

Mia glanced down at her fidgeting fingers.

What was she nervous about not telling me? "Does this have something to do with her telling me she punishes and rewards people for their behavior?"

Mia half-smiled. "Something like that. It's her story to tell, not mine."

These cryptic comments and half-conversations would drive me batty. I nodded rather than demand she tell me. It wouldn't do any good.

"We are in the best position to address Mark Mammon," Mia said. "Please reconsider joining us. For real."

"I'll think about it." And I would. Between my wonky premonitions and my misinterpretations of them, this had become more complicated than maybe it needed to be. I wondered what would come next.

CHAPTER SIXTEEN

"Good grief, my place is starting to feel as busy as The Strip," I quipped at the man standing in my doorway the next morning. "What can I do for you, Mark?"

"May I come in?"

"I don't think that's a good idea."

If it was possible, his black eyes darkened. "I saw your interview."

"And?"

"Seems risky to throw me under the bus like that."

"Pun intended?"

He flashed a wicked grin. "Why would you do that?"

"All's fair in love and war."

"We're at war?"

"We're not in love."

"Not yet."

I belly laughed. "Are you trying to seduce me?"

His smile turned enigmatic. "This is a conversation better had away from prying eyes and ears."

I leaned out past him and looked in the direction of my neighbors' homes. "I doubt anybody cares one way or the other." I sighed. "Fine, come on in."

Seated once again on my couch, entertaining a visitor, I waited for him to state his purpose. We stared at each other, and a strong sense of déjà vu rocked me. What was it with all these folks and their meaningful glances? "What do you want?"

"To win the election."

"Why?"

"Why, what?"

"Why do you want to win this election? Why Las Vegas? Why now? You've been around over 2000 years. If you want power, there are larger regions."

A look of consternation flashed across his face. "Someone's done their research."

"Mm-hmm." No reason to tell him Olivia told me that little tidbit.

"I don't want so much power that I draw unwanted attention," he answered.

"That's it?"

"What's your plan?" he asked instead.

I cocked an eyebrow at him. "To win the election."

"Touché." He laughed. "That's all?"

"What else is there?"

"What about seeing me punished for what I did?"

Mia's visit and entreaty to rejoin them flitted through my mind. "You mean my throwing you under the bus, as you so quaintly put it?"

"Yes." His smile dropped.

"I don't care about any of that," I lied.

"Really?"

"I said what I needed to in order to knock you down a few pegs in the polls. With only two days left before the election, I'm giving the citizens something negative about you." I shrugged. "That's all."

Now Mark quirked an eyebrow. "That's all? Why don't I believe that?"

"Because you're not a very trusting demon?"

He chuckled. "Listen, Barbara. I don't know what the group—"

"Group?"

He waved his hand dismissively. "The ones connected to that talent agency." He looked baffled by the idea of an investigative talent agency and I snorted.

"They're more effective than you might think," I mumbled.

"Anyway, I don't know what they've told you. But they lied."

"If you don't know what they've told me, then how do you know they lied?" I thought my question was rather obvious. Still, Mark's face darkened.

"I can imagine what they've said."

"And you're here, why? To correct the misinformation?"

"They probably told you that Olivia could take care of me, right?" His triumphant smirk told me my shock showed on my face. "They did."

I nodded.

"They're lying."

"They are?"

"Did they tell you who – or rather, what – Olivia is?"

Curiosity got the better of me. "No, they didn't, actually. I presume you know?"

"She's an archangel."

My eyes widened and I leaned back against the couch. "Wow."

"You know what this means, right?"

"Of course," I snapped. "She can send beings to Hell." I slyly smiled. "That's what they meant, then. Olivia will send you back to Hell once they can prove you killed those people."

His face tightened. "Or, they'll send you back."

Blood drained from my face. "They wouldn't."

"Are you sure?"

"They're after you."

"This time. What happens when you do something they don't like?" He stayed silent, no doubt watching the emotions play out across my face.

Was this all a trap? Would Olivia send me to Hell after taking care of Mark? As punishment for trying to get my former minion Robin to kill Jackson? Or even for hiring Olivia to kill Mark? Would Liam go along with that?

"You're here to convince me to work with you, so neither of us gets sent to Hell?" I clarified.

"Yes. I have a plan, but it will only work with your help."

"I'm listening."

"You need to mislead the talent agency group for two more days."

"Until after the election."

"Then, regardless of outcome, you and I can run the paranormal underworld together."

"We're supposed to trust each other?"

"We both have everything to lose if we don't."

"Until the election," I corrected. "Once one of us loses, the winner could easily choose to disregard this agreement."

He frowned. I was genuinely surprised that had not occurred to him. His face smoothed out. "We could make a pact."

Now I frowned. I had never made a pact with a fellow demon before, and wasn't entirely sure how they worked. "I'm not comfortable with that."

"Then what do you suggest?"

"We'll just have to trust each other."

"Sure, I can do that," he said easily.

I hoped I wasn't making another mistake, but holding onto my power was my destiny. I gave up so much, suffered in Hell even, for my destiny. And if I had to make a verbal agreement with another demon to hold on to my power, then so be it. Besides, it stung that the Paranormal Talent Agency group lied to me about Olivia. I couldn't trust them; why not throw my hat in the ring with Mark? I nodded my agreement.

"Here's my plan," he stated, and laid out the next couple of days.

CHAPTER SEVENTEEN

"Thank you all for coming," I greeted the group scattered around my living room, seated on the couch, and chairs brought in from the kitchen. Mark had left an hour earlier after I made my flurry of calls and texts. Liam, Catherine, Mia, Jacob, Jackson, and Olivia stared at me. No Evie, of course; daylight didn't mix well with vampires.

"What is this about?" Catherine asked.

"I met with Mark today." I ignored the gasps in response and held up my hands. "It's not what you think." Well, actually, it was undoubtedly exactly what they thought. Time to disabuse them of that. The best lies contained mostly truth. "He showed up here unannounced."

Liam watched me with hooded eyes.

"He asked me to join him against you."

"What did you tell him?" Mia asked.

"I countered by asking why I should join with him. I wanted to get an idea of his game plan."

"How did that go?" Jacob asked.

"He offered for us to team together to mislead you and, whatever the actual outcome of the election, we'd rule the underworld together."

"Interesting," Robin commented. I looked at her for more. She remained silent, only exchanging a glance with Jackson.

I made eye contact with Liam. This next piece was critical. "He told me that Olivia had the power to send him to Hell and that he assumed that was your plan."

"He did?" Liam asked.

"He did. I was surprised to hear that Olivia was an archangel." I took a calming breath before my eyes glowed red, and switched my gaze to the archangel in question.

"We planned on telling you, Barbara," Olivia explained.

"You did?"

"Yes. Honestly, we weren't sure if you were aligned with us or not," Mia answered.

"Well, after I recovered from my shock, I asked Mark how I could trust him."

"He did try to kill you," Jackson pointed out.

"Not really. He knew the crash wouldn't kill me. But, he had no real answer regarding me trusting him."

"How did the conversation end?" Liam asked this, his casual tone seemingly forced.

"I told him I couldn't trust him and that if I were him, I'd leave town before Olivia had the chance to send him to Hell."

Olivia leaned forward in her chair. "What was his response?"

"At first he tried to argue that he was safe because you couldn't prove he had done anything wrong."

"This isn't a court of law," Jacob commented with a shake of his head.

Olivia was nodding. "True, Jacob, but you all know that Mark is right. Without true belief in his guilt, I am unable to do anything."

"What about past wrongdoings?" Catherine asked.

"That gets complicated," Olivia side-stepped. She looked at me to continue.

"I told him that I intended to assist you in bringing him down. Literally," I added with a twisted smile. "He didn't like that and decided being here wasn't worth all this trouble."

"He did?" Catherine asked, her mouth dropping open.

"He did. I think he's planning on approaching New York. Bigger market and all that," I added.

"Just like the entertainment industry," Catherine chimed in with a laugh. "Sorry, occupational hazard."

"What does everybody think?" Jacob asked the group.

Brows furrowed, frowns surfaced, and several sets of shoulders shrugged. They were definitely not sure. Of me.

Of what Mark allegedly said. I caught myself tapping my fingers against my thigh and stilled them. I couldn't appear uncertain. I waited them out. It was important that they came to this conclusion on their own.

Mark and I had agreed we wanted to buy ourselves some time until the election. If they believed he left town, the little group would disband. And once he and I shared the power, we'd be unstoppable.

Power was my destiny; and my visions told me repeatedly that for my future, even if the details weren't clear, I needed to remain in power.

"Okay," Olivia said. "For now, we should operate as if this is true."

I bristled at the implication, though wasn't too irritated, since technically, I was lying and she shouldn't trust me. Oh the tangled webs we weave.

"Will you be leaving town then?" I asked. Olivia gave me an odd look and I hurried to clarify. "To go to New York after Mark?"

"Not just yet," she answered slowly. "I'll wait and see how the election goes."

Disappointment hit me. Mark and I had hoped that once she believed he'd left town, that she'd follow after.

"Is that a problem?"

"Of course not, Olivia. I would just hate for you to waste your time."

"How magnanimous," Robin sniped.

I glared at her. She needed to get over the whole minion thing; she'd willingly signed the pact with me, I didn't force her.

"It makes sense," Jackson commented. "Since his name is still on the ballot. He could have lied to you. Giving you the benefit of the doubt that you're telling the truth."

I nodded; how to spin this? I wasn't going to convince Olivia to leave, so I needed to show I supported the group. "You're absolutely correct. This late in the election cycle, there's no legal way to remove any names from the ballot. Makes complete sense to just wait."

"Thanks for letting us know," Mia said. "And thanks for joining back with us."

A flurry of guilt rose at her genuineness. "I like to pick the winning side." I ignored Robin rolling her eyes at the comment.

Jacob stood. "Thank you, Councilwoman. We'll be in touch." At this clear signal to the others, they stood and, after putting chairs back in the kitchen, headed en masse toward my front door. Liam held back some. I wondered why.

After the others exited, Liam paused at the door. His foot tapped, a sure sign of his nervousness.

"Did you want to stay?"

Liam wordlessly closed the door and walked to my kitchen table. He waited for me to take a seat before joining me.

"I know this is hard for you," he began.

You have no idea, I thought, but didn't say. "Hmm-mm."

"I caught your little joke at the end, about the winning side."

"That wasn't really a joke."

Liam reached for my hands and I let him. "Maybe not. You're still trying to come back."

"I am?"

"Don't you see that." The earnestness in his tone reignited my guilt over lying. "After all this time, you're starting back down the path of good. Don't you remember the beginning?"

"The 1500s were a long time ago," I said, biting my lip.

Liam chuckled. "They were; and a long way away."

"Not anymore," I corrected. "They have nonstop flights from Las Vegas to Ireland daily now." We shared small smiles.

"You gave your life to save others," he continued, voice straining as he tried to convince me of his argument.

I shook my head, yet didn't remove my hands from the warmth and comfort of his. That day in the village, protecting the children from the marauders, was so long ago. I couldn't lie and say I didn't remember the feeling of dying, Liam dying by my side, bleeding from multiple stab wounds. Then the love of the white light that made me an angel. Liam squeezed my hand in the present.

"Yes. You did, and you are. I know it feels foreign. It'll come back to you."

"It will?" I whispered.

"It's like riding a bike."

"Which I've never done."

"Never?"

"I've been busy."

"Consolidating power," he said, unable to disguise the bitterness. His fingers tightened on mine.

"Something like that," I agreed. Turned out the wish for power hurt when you got cast down to Hell. But only briefly.

"Maybe."

"Yes?" I didn't understand his comment.

"Maybe, when this is all over, we could try again."

My heart soared at the statement. Then it fell down to earth. I shook my head again. "Let's not rehash that old argument. I made my choice."

Liam stroked my jawline with his knuckles. "You did, once. Yes. But you don't have to make the same choice again. You're already making different choices than you have in the past," he insisted.

"True." I leaned my head into his fingers, enjoying the feel of his skin on mine. "Maybe," I finally agreed and a wide smile lit up his face. I thought he might kiss me. Instead, he released me and stood.

"Let's wrap this up so we can move forward."

I nodded, not trusting myself to speak, and followed him to the door. When it closed behind him, I leaned my forehead against the cool wood.

What was I doing?

Could Liam and I really turn back time and try again?

Was Mark lying to me about Olivia?

No, the Paranormal Talent Agency folks confirmed she could send both of us back to Hell.

I had to protect myself. Even if it cost me my heart.

I'd stick with the plan. While it was disappointing that Olivia wasn't leaving town, that didn't change anything. Tomorrow morning, Mark would launch the second step.

CHAPTER EIGHTEEN

"Good morning in the Valley," Elizabeth Addison's cheerful voice greeted viewers to her morning show, *Entertainment Daily*. I lounged on my couch, cup of coffee in hand – black, of course. The camera panned to show a man in a sharp charcoal suit sitting in a blue chair across from Elizabeth. The camera panned back to her now-solemn face.

"As many of you know, Mark Mammon is running against Councilwoman Barbara Knollman for the position of Mayor. The councilwoman came on this show and implied certain things about Mr. Mammon. He is here today to set the record straight." She turned to face him and nodded. "Mr. Mammon, what do you want the viewers to know?"

"First, thank you for allowing me this opportunity to clear the air. And, second, thank you for supporting this city with everything you do." Elizabeth preened at the praise and I rolled my eyes. Oh, get on with it, Mark!

Mark stared into the camera lens, which obligingly zoomed in on his handsome face. "Let me start by saying that this is not an attack on the Councilwoman," he began. "She's as much a victim in all of this as I am." He straightened his not-crooked tie and thinned his lips. "This pains me to say. The bus crash that killed the other candidates was intended for me." His eyes glistened as if fighting back tears.

"Without providing details—" He held up his hand to stop Elizabeth from asking any questions. "—in order to preserve the ongoing investigation, I have been targeted. And lives have been lost as a result. Because of this, I debated dropping out of the race entirely. I would hate for something to happen to the Councilwoman in an attempt to get to me.

"But," and his eyes became steel, "I will not hide from those seeking to harm me. I know I would be good for this city. And whether the citizens of Las Vegas vote for me tomorrow or not, I want them to have that choice. So many of their choices have already been taken away."

The camera switched to Elizabeth. I chuckled at her jaw dropped open. She snapped her mouth closed and smiled grimly. "And, there you have it folks. These are sinister times." The camera pulled back; Mark opened his mouth to speak. Elizabeth jumped in with a finger raised.

"Just one more thing, Mr. Mammon. What does all of this have to do with the paranormal underworld?" She smiled sweetly.

He floundered in his response. "I'm not sure I understand the question."

"I know you're newer to Las Vegas, but you may have heard about my series of exposés regarding the supernatural beings that call Vegas home."

He nodded.

"I've heard unsubstantiated whispers that the city council has something to do with the local governance of these beings."

Having figured out where Elizabeth was going, Mark recovered. "I wouldn't know anything about that, Elizabeth," he responded, voice slick as an oil field.

"Are you denying that there's a connection between the supernatural underworld, the acting industry, and the city council?" she pushed, all traces of a smile vanished. The brunette human could certainly be tenacious.

"I do not," he enunciated. "I simply wish for the opportunity to guide my adopted home to the greatest heights possible."

Elizabeth swung her head to face the nearest camera and grinned. "As many questions as answers. Don't forget to tune in on Friday for my latest *Mythical Being of the Week* segment. Have a wonderful day in the Valley," she signed off and a commercial played.

I wasn't sure what impact those last questions would have, but Mark put on a great show. I figured he'd call in about a minute. I set my coffee mug down on the table just as my phone rang. Perfectly predictable.

"Do you know where that human was going with those questions?"

No social niceties, I saw. "I don't. She exposed aspects of the supernatural underworld last year. And as she mentioned, she does that weekly show. That's all I know."

Mark remained silent. I waited him out. "I wasn't expecting those," he finally admitted.

"That was obvious."

"Gee, thanks."

"You covered well though. After."

"Thanks for throwing me a bone."

"I'm not your cheerleader."

"Definitely not." He chuckled. "You know you're in more danger now."

My attention sharpened. "What do you mean?"

"Even if they didn't watch, I'm sure word will get to that acting group quickly."

"And?"

"They'll think you lied to them about me dropping out of the race."

"In point of fact, I did lie to them," I responded with a laugh. "I'm not worried. They'll more likely just think *you* lied to me. Not that I lied to them."

"What if you're wrong?"

"What's the worst they can do?"

"Olivia can send you to Hell."

"For lying?"

"For evidence that you're connected to me, a killer."

"Right." I frowned. "What do you suggest?"

"Strike first."

"Excuse me?"

"Take care of Liam and Olivia."

I was sure I misheard him. "Did you just say I should kill Liam and Olivia?"

He ignored my question. "Certain steps need to be taken to secure our future."

"Don't you think that's a bit of jumping the shark?"

"This isn't a television show, so I wouldn't worry about it." I heard the grin in his voice.

At least he understood my reference, I groused silently. "Still, it seems unnecessarily dramatic," I argued.

"Do what you want, of course. But, if I'm right..." He trailed off to allow me to fill in the blanks.

"Fine, I'll do it."

"I'm on my way."

"Why?"

"Just in case you need me."

"Why would I need you?"

"What if one of them tries something? Don't you want back-up?"

"Fine," I agreed wearily. "Let's get this over with."

The call disconnected and I stewed in my uncertainty. Was this the right choice? I was a demon after all. Isn't this what we did? Frankly, it was amazing I had made it hundreds of years without killing anyone. Of course, that was because of the power of my premonitions. I frowned and dialed Liam's number. In an hour this would all be over.

CHAPTER NINETEEN

I swung my door open and glared at Mark. He sauntered past me like he owned the place. His overconfidence rankled.

"Make yourself at home."

"I will."

I followed him to the living room and we stood next to the couch. His eyes cut to the revolver on the coffee table and he cocked an eyebrow.

"I decided to go old school," I answered his unasked question with a shrug. Inside, my heart was racing. I could still call this off.

He nodded. "That'll work. Enchanted bullets, I assume?"

"I've had them on hand for years. Never thought I'd actually use them," I answered, though the latter seemed directed more at myself.

"I like it. We can concoct a story about them breaking in and you shooting them in self-defense." He looked around the room. "I'll wait in the bedroom, just in case you need me. But it looks like you're good. How soon will they arrive?"

I glanced at my watch. "Liam will arrive in thirty and Olivia about twenty after that." He frowned. "Did you have somewhere else you needed to be?" His frown deepened at my sarcasm.

"I don't like the delay. They could be planning something."

"I doubt it."

Mark searched my face for a moment before shrugging and smiling. "I'll be in the bedroom, then." He waggled his eyebrows at me and I raised one in return.

"Are you flirting?"

"Not at all," he called over his shoulder as he left the room.

I took my seat on the couch and picked up the gun. It felt heavy in my hands. I knew how to shoot, had learned a long time ago. It had been awhile, though. I hoped it would come back to me. Would this also be like riding a bike, to use Liam's phrase? I pointed the gun forward, sighted the other end of the room. They were arriving separately so I wouldn't have to get off two shots in rapid succession. How close would they need to get for me to increase my chance of a kill with the first shots?

My hands trembled and I lowered the gun to my lap. Maybe they were planning something. If they spoke to each other and realized I requested to see them separately, would they know something was up?

I swallowed past a large lump in my throat. Who was I kidding? I wasn't trembling due to nervousness about them. I was trembling because that voice in the back of my head wouldn't stop screaming that this was the wrong path. Why was I trusting Mark? Why did I believe him that the group would be planning to send us both to Hell? Liam wouldn't do that.

Liam.

My heart constricted at the thought of his death. Especially at my hands. I had loved him once. I inwardly groaned. I loved him still. They say you never forget your first love, especially if it began when you were only teenagers. We'd been like star-crossed lovers; except for instead of staying dead after the invaders killed us during the attack on our village, Liam and I had been elevated to angels for giving our lives to protect others. If we still had a chance…

I shook my head. No, I'd stick with the plan. Swirling mist formed in front of me and I frantically tried to stop it in my head. I wasn't successful. I slumped back against the couch and the vision formed.

I almost groaned aloud when I saw the familiar form of the back of the dark-haired man. Except something new.

He put one hand behind his head and rubbed at the base of his neck. Now I did gasp. That was Liam, not Mark. He began to walk away and the image shifted to Olivia again, bright blue eyes flashing – angrily? – at me. She shook her head, then looked over her shoulder at the retreating form of Liam. When she looked at me again, her eyes glistened with unshed tears. The image vanished and I sat up, wide-eyed.

"I've been wrong this entire time." The words came out a whisper. As I continued, they strengthened. "The feeling of betrayal was me betraying Liam for false power. Love is my destiny. He came back into my life to help me see that." Peace settled over me for the first time since this whole mess began and I knew I finally had it right. "What is wrong with me?"

"Did you say something?" Mark asked from the bedroom.

"I know I'm a demon, but could demons have love too?" I continued in a whisper.

Mark's voice, closer now. "What are you mumbling about?" He must have come out of the bedroom. "Liam'll be here any minute."

I made eye contact with the demon now standing fifteen feet away. I set the gun on the coffee table and stood to face him. "I can't do it."

Mark's eyes glowed red.

CHAPTER TWENTY

The doorbell chimed. I couldn't pull my gaze from Mark's glowing red eyes. He smiled cruelly before turning to walk back to the bedroom. "You will follow the plan." I tried to take a step toward him and deliver an angry retort, but found myself unable to do so.

"What are you doing to me?" I managed to ask this before realizing I no longer controlled my actions. I leaned down to pick up the gun.

The door slammed open with a crash. Liam rushed into the living room.

I pointed the gun at Liam and he held his hands up.

"You're choosing this again?"

I opened my mouth, and could not speak. What was wrong with me? It felt like someone was pulling marionette strings and I had become the puppet. I took a step toward Liam.

Disappointment shone in his eyes. "I thought you were choosing a new path."

Tears filled my eyes. I still couldn't speak.

"You don't have to do this."

With every ounce of willpower I had, I ordered my arm to lower. It shook but did not comply. Liam noticed the movement.

"Barbara, there's still a chance for you. For us."

Tears spilled out of my eyes. Still my arm did not lower.

"I've missed you," Liam whispered. "I thought maybe this time…"

I still didn't respond and his expression hardened. "You chose the power of a demon once before."

I cocked the weapon, my arm steady, despite my renewed attempts to lower it. Anxiety zinged through me. What was going on?

"Wasn't losing your angel status enough. Is power really worth all this?" His voice softened, desperation saturating the words. "Do you really want to return to Hell?"

My finger started to pull the trigger. Liam's eyes widened and the fierce love I had for the angel standing before me surged. I released the trigger and opened my mouth.

"He's controlling me. I can't fight him. He's in the bedroom." I swung the gun away from Liam as my finger pulled the trigger. The bullet shattered a window, glass tinkling when it hit the hard floor. The recoil shoved my shoulder back and the sound was loud in the enclosed space. Liam's eyes cut to behind me.

Liam raced past. My arm holding the gun dropped and I turned to see an enraged Mark emerging from the bedroom. His focus on Liam meant he released me from his hold. Liam raised a fist to punch Mark, but froze. Mental manipulation. Mark had an active power after all.

Mark walked up to Liam and leaned in to whisper. "You think you had this all figured out." Mark glared at me, then a smile split his face. "You, on the other hand, are much stronger than I gave you credit for. Maybe I won't kill you when this is all over."

I started to raise the gun and he wagged his finger at me.

"Don't do it. I may change my mind again and kill you after all."

I hesitated. Was I fast enough to raise the gun and shoot him before he could grab my mind again? If I did, would that give Liam enough time to stop him?

I raised the gun and Mark turned the full force of his power on me. I cried out at the mental invasion. It was like an alien presence in my brain.

Liam pounced, grabbing Mark in a bear hug. The distraction broke Mark's hold over me and I trained the gun on the grappling men. I couldn't get a good shot. Liam got several good hits in – and it was weird to see supernatural beings engaging in fisticuffs, I'll be honest – before freezing again. Mark decked him and Liam slumped to the ground. My arm froze halfway up and Mark smiled lazily at me. He knew he had won.

He stalked toward me like a lion approaching a gazelle. His finger reached out to brush my cheek. He shook his head. "It's too bad. We might have worked well together."

Motion at the front door drew my attention. Olivia had arrived.

CHAPTER TWENTY-ONE

Olivia walked in, absorbing the scene before her. She trained her sights on Mark, ignoring me with the gun. As if she knew…

"Release her," she commanded.

Mark's face contorted but he did not comply.

"Is this how you did it?" My question snuck out during his lapse in concentration. When Olivia looked at me, I realized I distracted her. Mark's eyes glowed red as he swung his head back and forth between me and Olivia. He sneered.

"Trying to keep me talking?"

"Don't you want to gloat," I taunted, "about how you've accomplished all of this under our noses?"

I could practically read his internal debate on his face. He shrugged. "Sure, why not? We have a minute." I noticed that although I could now speak and control myself, Olivia's face had taken on a strained look. Was he controlling her now? He was right. I needed to keep him talking while I figured out if I had enough time to stop him.

When I gestured for him to continue, he grinned. "Yes, this is how I did it. You've seen my power."

"Mental manipulation."

"Mind control. Mental manipulation. You can call it whatever you like. It's effective."

"How did you crash the bus?"

His gaze flicked between me and the frozen Olivia again. "Who has the most control in an accident?"

"The driver."

"Exactly."

My mouth gaped open. "You weren't anywhere near the driver. How could you—"

"I have a long reach," he interrupted my question, the answer a clear threat. He sighed with a shake of his head. "Caesar never understood that, either."

My eyes squinted in confusion. "Caesar? Julius Caesar?" Olivia had said they'd known each other.

Mark chortled. "He wouldn't listen to me, either. So, I took care of him."

My eyes widened. "His own men stabbed him to death," I contradicted.

He cocked an eyebrow. "Did they?"

"Understood." I raised the gun slightly and Mark tilted his head.

"You do understand. I killed the others. You're the last candidate left. When you kill them—" He gestured toward the prone Liam and frozen Olivia. "—that takes care of the Olivia problem. You get arrested and I win the election. Don't worry," he added in a conciliatory tone. "I'll allow you to escape. As long as you leave my jurisdiction."

I nodded. "I can do that." I frowned. "I'm confused about one point."

"Yes?"

"This really can't be all about the Las Vegas region. I know that's what you told me before, but…"

Mark eyed me, made some internal decision. "You're very perceptive, Barbara. This was never about Las Vegas."

"Never?"

His eyes burned in Olivia's direction. "It was always about her. The only being left who could send me back to Hell." I gaped and he focused on me. "I needed help. I needed a distraction. Your silly election did the trick."

My silly election? I formulated my plan. I raised the gun the rest of the way, pointed at Olivia. A calm settled over me. It was now or never. My arm swung toward Mark. He snarled and his control enveloped me. My arm dropped.

It was enough.

"That's all I needed to hear," Olivia stated and strode toward him.

The glowing in Mark's eyes increased exponentially. It hurt to look at him, so I turned my face toward Olivia.

She held her arms outstretched toward him. The glowing bathed her in an unnatural red light but she seemed unaffected.

Mark emitted an inhuman growl, drawing my attention. He raised his own hands.

I started to raise my arm again.

"Don't," came Liam's weak voice from the floor. "Don't."

A white light flowed from Olivia's hands and wrapped itself around Mark like a cobra. It darkened, becoming blue, then violet, and finally a pulsing red. The light appeared alive, but it couldn't be.

Mark's skin rippled, the glow from his eyes dimmed. He dropped his hands, futilely pulling at the strands of light surrounding him. His skin disintegrated showing the beast beneath, only for a moment, before he collapsed to the floor and winked out of existence.

I fully faced Olivia. "You did it. You sent him to Hell," I said, awestruck.

She turned her glowing white eyes toward me and my legs became jelly. I looked to Liam, who was now standing, with a sorrowful expression on his face. He couldn't save me. And I wouldn't ask him to. The gun fell to the floor beside me. I closed my eyes.

"Do it," I told the avenging angel. "I deserve it."

I hoped it wouldn't hurt too much.

CHAPTER TWENTY-TWO

Nothing happened. I opened one eye a slit. Olivia's eyes had returned to their startling shade of blue. She was looking at me with compassion.

Compassion?

"You can open your eyes, Barbara."

I did. "You aren't going to send me to Hell?"

"Do you want me to?"

I seriously considered the question. "No, I don't. Why don't you?"

Olivia crossed the room and took my hands in hers. Light tingling ran up my arms. She released my hands with a chuckle. "Sorry about that. Residual energy."

"I allied myself with Mark. More than once."

"True," she agreed. "But you were different. Are different."

"How so?"

"He was only concerned with himself."

"And that's different from me how?" I heard the bitterness in my voice.

"You had second doubts from the beginning."

"Yes. But, look what I almost did," I whispered, my arm sweeping to encompass the room. I made the mistake of meeting Liam's eyes. They were blank. Whatever feelings we might have been rekindling had vanished.

"But, you didn't," Olivia gently reminded me.

I sunk down onto the couch and buried my head in my hands. "Did you know?"

"That I was his target? Yes."

"How?"

"I've been after him for… some time now," she said with a chuckle. "Whenever I'd get close, he'd go underground or the evidence would magically vanish. He's one of the last elder demons."

"There's a hierarchy?" I snort laughed. "Bureaucracy everywhere."

"I was going to get him eventually. When I heard he was on the ballot, the only rational reason I could think of was that he wanted me to know."

"And the only reason he'd want that would be if he had a plan to take care of you," I completed the thought.

"Exactly."

I frowned. "How could he know I would contact you? Am I that predictable?"

"My guess is he had a backup plan in case you didn't. He probably knew you'd protected me last year."

"Not that you needed protection."

She grinned. "You didn't know that. And Mark thought he was strong enough to manipulate you."

"He was," I said in a small voice.

"Not in the end. He couldn't hold you. You didn't shoot me. I was able to get my confession. You helped with that, Barbara."

I raised my head and nodded. "I did."

"And you didn't have to."

"I didn't." My voice sounded stronger. Maybe this would be okay after all.

"You'll be fine, Barbara," Olivia assured me. "I have to go. Paperwork to file."

"I remember angel bureaucracy. I can only imagine it's exponentially worse as an archangel." We shared a smile.

"Liam, I'll be in touch." And with that, she left.

Liam started to follow, without a glance at me.

"Wait."

He turned, that blank expression still lodged on his face. "Yes?"

"Can we talk?"

A grimace of pain indicated the crack in his façade. The act of speaking appeared difficult. "This might be too much. I thought you turned a corner. Now…"

Tears filled my eyes. "It's too late?"

"I can't, I won't, go down that path again with you." With a sorrowful shake of his head, he continued walking toward my front door.

"Goodbye, Barbara."

A heart I didn't think could still love shattered into a million pieces. After all this time, I finally chose the right path. It was too late. I lost my love. Again.

CHAPTER TWENTY-THREE

The next morning dawned far too beautiful for my mood. April in Las Vegas could be so wonderful. It was the day of the election. Such a tortured twisted road to get here. And I no longer really cared.

I trudged through my morning routine, running through the expectations for Candidate Barbara Knollman. A glance at my clock confirmed I still had a few hours before I was expected at campaign headquarters for monitoring the voting returns.

My mind swirled with the choices I'd made over the past months, years, decades even, but most importantly the past week. So many opportunities to choose the right path. I couldn't fully blame it on misunderstanding my premonitions. They were never clear cut; I knew a being's personality filtered the interpretation of them. Had I continually interpreted them to support my desire for power? Apparently so. And what had that gotten me? Well, I was probably about to win the mayor's seat. There was that.

I stepped out of the shower and grabbed a towel. What could be my next steps? Assuming I won – fairly clear-cut, I mused, given I was the only candidate still alive – maybe I could focus on improving the image of supernaturals, now that humanity knew of our existence. This energized me some.

If I couldn't have love, I could use my powers for good. I barked a laugh in my empty kitchen. A demon doing good. Would wonders never cease.

Breakfast consisted of whatever I had on hand, I didn't even pay attention. Soon I was heading to campaign headquarters. Although not expected for another couple of hours, I didn't want to sit home alone in my sterile house, staring at the walls.

I pulled open the door to the building, catching sight of busy-bee volunteers manning phones and chatting with each other. They were excited, though I wasn't sure how known it was that I was the only candidate left.

"Are you okay?" Lynn Fox, my campaign manager greeted me just inside the door, her expression concerned behind her red-rimmed glasses.

"Why do you ask?"

"Elizabeth Addison mentioned on her show this morning that Mammon was killed – and you were present."

"She did, huh?"

Lynn frowned. "Yes. What happened?"

I debated how to answer, before deciding on a half-truth. "He came to my home, threatening me and several members of the entertainment industry. He was… eliminated. Self-defense?" My inflection suggested I wasn't so sure of that and Lynn's eyebrows rose. She recovered quickly.

"I'm glad you're okay," she stated. "The upside of the crazy last week is that you're the only candidate left. You've got it in the bag."

"Unless they pick None of the Above," I quipped.

Lynn bit back a laugh at my joke. "I doubt they'll do that."

I smiled. "No, I don't think they will."

"What would you like to do?" She glanced at her watch. Results wouldn't be coming in for quite a while, so she probably didn't know what to do with me.

"I'd like to chat with the volunteers about how this election has been for them and what they'd like me to focus on when I win."

Lynn couldn't cover her surprise fast enough. If my disinterest in my constituency had been this obvious, how on earth did I keep getting volunteers, let alone winning elections?

"That'd be great, Madam Councilwoman. Follow me." She turned and I followed.

The next hours passed in a blur of getting to know the various volunteers that I had only smiled at and said hello to in the past. It was gratifying to hear from them what they'd enjoyed and what they'd like to see from me. I could also tell they were happy I was asking their opinions. Why hadn't I done this sooner?

"Okay, everybody, it looks like FOX5 is about to call the election," Lynn announced late that evening. We'd pulled the uncomfortable metal folding chairs around the large flat screen television in one corner of the space. Volunteers munched on finger food. Excitement was palpable in the air. This was kind of fun.

The camera framed Elizabeth Addison following a local car commercial. Her brown hair shined under the lights and she wore her anchor expression. I inwardly laughed; sometimes it seemed she was the only newscaster in town!

"Welcome back to our continuing coverage of the primary elections for the mayor and open city council seats. We'll get to the other seats in a moment. Not surprisingly, we are able to call the election for Mayor. As the only remaining candidate alive, we can confidently state that Barbara Knollman has won in a landslide and will be your new Mayor."

Elizabeth continued to talk, but the cheering volunteers around me drowned her out. People patted me on the back and hugged each other. Congratulations floated around the room. Lynn leaned in to me.

"Congratulations, ma'am," she said with a wide smile.

"Speech, speech, speech." The chanting rose in volume. I noticed a couple of cameramen filming us, the reporters standing just off to the side.

I fixed a smile on my face and held my hands up to silence the crowd. They complied. The cameras and reporters moved in closer.

"Thank you all for all of your hard work. It paid off." Cheers rose again from the crowd, and then silenced. "I would not be here tonight if not for the many people working tirelessly behind the scenes on my behalf.

"Thank you, first and foremost, to Lynn Fox, my campaign manager." I turned toward her. "You kept me going and focused on the right things, right up to the end." I was piling the manure a little high, but it was expected. I then proceeded to thank some of the lead volunteers, and the group more generally. After the applause died down, I paused, my smile dipping for a moment. Tension increased in the room.

"For the past months, a new world has been identified here in Las Vegas," I started, my voice quiet, though building steam. "What has been dubbed the paranormal underworld." I ignored the gasps from the audience. I was way off-book.

"I am familiar with this underworld." The gasps were louder. "I plan to ask Elizabeth Addison to have me on her show tomorrow morning, to discuss the rumors and misinformation that has been swirling for these past months. I hope you will all tune in. Thank you." You could hear a pin drop in the absolute silence that followed my statement.

I nodded at the crowd, at Lynn, and strode to the back office, the blood pounding in my head. This was a bold move. I heard my cellphone vibrating on the desk.

I closed the door behind me and answered my phone. "Hi, Liam."

"That was some speech."

"Did you like it?"

"I have mixed feelings. What are you playing at?"

That stung. "I'm not playing. Supernatural creatures are only nominally out of the closet. I aim to change that."

"Why?"

"What do you mean, why?"

"What's in it for you?"

"That's unnecessarily harsh," I snapped, then softened my tone. "I told you. I'm making new choices now. I had a premonition last year—" I stopped. Mist had begun swirling before me.

"Barbara?"

"Liam, I have to go." I ended the call, vaguely aware he was still speaking. I closed my eyes to focus on the image forming.

A dark-haired man, seen from behind, though I knew without question it was Liam. The man turned to face me, his face open yet questioning. He looked to the side and Catherine came into view. I wondered if this was related to me thinking about the prior premonition. Liam nodded at Catherine, who seemed perplexed. She closed her eyes and when she opened them, I gasped.

White light glowed from within Catherine. Liam nodded and seemed to stare at me. He approached, reached out a hand. Even though premonitions didn't come with tactile sensations, I swore I could feel his fingers on my cheek. He smiled, nodded again at Catherine, and turned away. I felt hollow as I watched him walk further and further until I could no longer see him.

Catherine blinked and the white light vanished. Peace surrounded her. That didn't make sense to me, yet I knew it to be true. She also smiled at me, then turned to follow Liam, walking until she too vanished from the premonition.

Where were they going? Why was Liam following Catherine? Was the premonition telling me he would be on her path?

Whatever that was.

I opened my eyes, and gasped when I saw Liam standing there, an uncertain expression on his face. I held onto that peace from the premonition and smiled at him.

"Is everything okay?" he asked, a frown playing on his lips.

"It's good that you came," I answered.

"It is?"

"I know what to do now."

CHAPTER TWENTY-FOUR

Liam stepped fully into the office and closed the door behind him. He hesitated.

"Please have a seat."

He did and we stared at each other for a beat.

"Putting aside your doubts about my motivation, what do you think about supernatural beings being more visible? Being truly considered in the world."

"I'm honestly not sure, given how humanity sometimes reacts to individuals different than themselves." He shrugged. "Remember the clashing that killed us hundreds of years ago. But, this may be the new way of things."

I nodded. "I agree. I believe there could, should, be more for us."

"What do you propose? What do you plan to say on the show tomorrow?"

"Let me back up a bit first."

He nodded.

"Last year, I had a premonition of the importance of Catherine Rodham to my future. Or what I thought was my future. I believe I misread that premonition."

"You do?"

I reddened. "I've been misreading a few of them of late," I admitted and a small smile formed on his face in response. "You realize I was experiencing another premonition when you arrived?"

"I assumed. I wasn't sure why you disconnected the call—"

"Were you worried about me?"

"Maybe." He coughed. "When I walked in, I recognized that blank stare," he hurried to add. The premonitions had started when we'd been given angel status, and Liam had watched me have them for a hundred years.

Oddly, they hadn't stopped when I'd been struck down as a demon after telling Liam in a fit of anger that I was tired of humanity and would rather pursue my own interests as a demon rather than continue as an angel. Maybe a piece of my angelic nature still remained.

I rather liked that thought, but that was a consideration for another day. I stilled my wandering thoughts and focused on his questioning expression.

"The premonition tonight also featured Catherine."

He quirked an eyebrow.

"I'm not entirely sure what it meant." I hesitated.

"But you have an idea?"

"I'm almost certain it is related to bringing the supernatural world fully into the realm of humanity."

"How come?"

I hesitated again. "I'd rather not say. In case I'm wrong again."

We shared a smile.

"There was more," I continued, tapping my nails on the desk. His expression told me he recognized my nervous fidgeting for what it was.

"Yes?"

"You were in the premonition." His eyes dilated, his desire surprising me.

"I was?" he asked.

"Yes." I dropped my gaze, gathering my courage. "My victory tonight was hollow." I raised my head. "I know one piece is what I plan to speak about tomorrow. However, the premonition tonight confirmed something else."

He remained silent.

"I love you." He frowned. Not the reaction I hoped for. "I've always loved you."

"Love was never our problem."

"I agree. My choice of power over love was. Has been." I cleared my throat. "I want to change that."

"How?"

"I know you said that you couldn't walk this path with me again. And, if that remains the case, I won't bother you further. If you're open to it… if it's not too late, I would like to try again. I made the wrong choice before. And I made the wrong choice with Mark. I won't blame it on my premonitions. Those were mine to interpret, and I chose interpretations that fit with my lust for power. But, when the announcement was made that I'd won tonight, I didn't care. My greed for power blinded me to what was real." I stopped.

"How do I know this isn't just a blip?" His words questioned. His open posture said he was listening.

"As a show of good faith, I'll resign my position as Mayor."

"You just won," he reminded me.

"I'd stay on long enough for a smooth transition. You're stalling."

"I am."

"Why?"

"My heart tells me to jump at this chance. My brain tells me I'll be burned again." He half-smiled. "No pun intended."

I belly laughed at the reference to my glowing eyes, startling Liam. "That's why I'm offering to resign. I want you to know that I'm all in this time. Forever."

"On one condition. Tell me why you changed your name to Barbara?"

"That's your condition?" I shrugged. "Having the name of a pagan goddess seemed wrong as a demon."

"I liked Brighid."

"As did I."

"I like Barbara, too," Liam admitted.

"I'm glad, since it'd be awkward to change it back at this point."

"Okay."

"Okay?"

He stood and walked around the chair to stand over me. His hand cupped my chin and I leaned in to the touch. "I'll accept that your name is Barbara, not Brighid, going forward."

"Is that all?" I whispered.

"It's not too late for us. I've been waiting hundreds of years for you to come to your senses."

"Even though I'm a demon?"

"What's a relationship if it doesn't have some challenges?"

I stood and we embraced, his warm arms encircling me. I inhaled his scent, reveling in how good he felt. "I'll let the Council know immediately of my resignation."

Liam held me at arms' length. "You don't need to resign."

I pulled fully away with a shake of my head. "I appreciate that, but I do. I don't want to be tempted down the wrong path again."

"I don't believe you will," he countered.

"You don't?"

"I don't. You haven't talked about helping others since you lost your angel status and became a demon. I believe you've truly turned over a new leaf with your goal of developing human-supernatural relations."

"As do I," came a female voice.

CHAPTER TWENTY-FIVE

Olivia stood five feet from us, in all her blue-haired archangel glory. She smiled benevolently. Somehow I wasn't surprised she could materialize. No wonder she'd never ridden on a private jet before, I thought with an internal chuckle. She walked toward us, so graceful she appeared to be gliding. Heck, maybe she was.

"You do, too?" I asked.

"I do."

"Why?"

"Besides the reasons Liam gave? Because I've been watching your evolution, and you're ready."

"You've been watching me?" I asked, ignoring the rest of her statement.

"Of course. When you chose power over love, I was the one who stripped you of your angel status and relegated you to living as a demon."

My hand flew to my mouth, but nothing emerged. My eyes cut to Liam's similarly surprised expression.

Olivia grinned. "Guess you guys didn't know that."

I shook my head.

"I also was the one who elevated you both," she said.

"That shapeless light Liam and I saw? That was you?"

"Yes, it was."

I met Liam's eyes. That light was the last thing either of us remembered before waking up as angels. Olivia really got around. I wondered idly how long she'd been around.

"This was always going to be your path," she continued.

"Destiny?"

"Something like that?"

"Don't we have free will like the humans?"

"Of course."

She didn't even hesitate stating these completely contradictory statements. I frowned.

"I know it doesn't make sense." The unspoken *to you* made me smile.

"I'll accept it as gospel."

Olivia snort laughed. "Nice."

"I'll be here all night."

"You've reached the point where it is time for a chance. Though—" She clasped her hands together. "—I don't know if I should tell you this."

"Please. At this point, I'd like to know everything I possibly can."

"You might not like it," she warned.

"What could be worse than existing as a demon worried about being sent back to Hell?"

"Ah, yes." She released her hands and played with the sides of her flowing sage dress.

"Is it that bad?"

She searched my face, found what she was looking for. "You always could have chosen a different path."

A sense of confused disappointment filled me at her statement. "Well, yes." Was I missing something?

"You always could have chosen love over power," she clarified.

I tilted my head, still not understanding.

"And restored your angel status."

The weight of her statement slammed into me and my breath caught in my throat. "I could have chosen love to become an angel again at any time." She nodded. "And by choosing love now, I can be restored to angel status?" I scarcely believed it possible. Although it pained me some that I had wasted all these years, until this exact point in time, I honestly never would have chosen a different path. I thought I had chosen the correct one all those years ago.

"What happens now?"

Olivia's eyes glowed white in response to my question. The light wrapped around me, and I cried out. Not from pain, but from the love enveloping me. The light became opaque; I existed in a shell of light. Rhythmic pulsing, pleasant and insistent, synched with the beat of my human heart. It slowed to a stop – was I dying? I didn't believe this had been a trick.

Before the question had fully formed, my heart started again. Slow, even beats. The light thinned and became translucent, before fading away. I stared through renewed eyes at Olivia and Liam. It was difficult to explain. My vision seemed clearer, everything seemed brighter. Even the air smelled better. My gaze flicked between the two.

"Am I an angel again?" I wondered if that meant I had regained my youthful appearance and my hazel eyes.

Olivia nodded and a single tear tracked down Liam's cheek. There was my answer.

"Welcome back, Barbara," Olivia hummed. Even my hearing was different. Crisper, yet softer. Was it like this when I was an angel before? I couldn't remember. The darkness of my demon existence crowded the rest out.

"Thank you," I whispered.

Olivia shook her head. "I merely did what was necessary. You made the choice."

"Thank you, anyway."

"You're welcome. Do you have any other questions?"

I started to shake my head no, then stopped. "Yes! In my premonitions, I saw Liam. I've figured out what that meant." Liam and I exchanged smiles. "I also saw Catherine Rodham. And, I saw her last year. She seems to be very important. Except I'm not sure what the premonitions mean. Last year, I thought she was important in my quest for power in this region." I held my hands up in question. "Now I have no idea."

"She was important in your… quest. Just not for power." Olivia smiled her Cheshire-cat grin. "And she remains important. Everyone is still on the right path and the end is nearly here."

"What does that—"

Olivia dematerialized before I could finish my question. "I guess I'll have to live without that answer." I looked at Liam and he shrugged.

"I have no idea. Archangels don't share the grand plan with lowly angels."

"You're not lowly," I teased while walking to him.

"We're equal now."

"Equally lowly, I guess."

"This has been a crazy ride." Liam took my hands in his, kissed the tops of both. He released them and leaned in for a hug, his fingers twining in my long full locks of chestnut brown hair that fell around my shoulders.

"It has," I whispered into his ear.

"Let's not worry about any grand plans today." He kissed my cheek, nibbled on my ear lobe.

"What should we think about?"

"Getting to know each other all over again," he said, his voice raspy with desire.

"That sounds like an excellent plan," I agreed.

His lips found mine, and I moaned in response. We had centuries of missed love to make up for.

128

EPILOGUE

Elizabeth Addison and I sat side by side on the familiar blue chairs on the set of *Entertainment Daily*. Her tilted head distracted me from romantic thoughts of Liam. I could tell she'd been wanting to ask me questions since I arrived. I was moderately impressed that she had so far contained herself. Of course, maybe she just wanted to surprise me once the cameras rolled.

I gave her my widest smile, which she mirrored before remembering she wasn't supposed to like me. After all, she wasn't privy to what had happened yesterday. It amazed me that everything happened only yesterday.

"In thirty, Liz," a faceless voice in the dark of the studio informed her.

When the countdown finished, Elizabeth flashed her perfect chicklet-teeth smile at the camera. "Good morning in the Valley! Welcome to *Entertainment Daily*. I'm your host, Elizabeth Addison." She leaned forward in the chair, like a co-conspirator. "I have a special treat for you this morning. As most of you know, yesterday Barbara Knollman won the election for Mayor of Las Vegas. Today, she is our guest." Elizabeth swung her gaze to mine and her smile became predatory.

"Let's get this first part out of the way," the host stated.

"Yes?" I knew where she was going but I wanted her to work for it.

"You look different."

"Hmm-mm. I do?"

"Don't be coy," she said, wagging her finger at me. She meant to be playful, I'm sure. "I know plastic surgery isn't that good, or that fast," Elizabeth commented with maximum snark.

I laughed, my laugh genuine and not rude. Her smirk faltered. "You are correct, Elizabeth. And, I'm not laughing at you. I promise." I took a deep breath. "I am different. That's part of why I'm here today."

"Tell the viewers everything," she encouraged.

"Do you know why I wanted to do my first interview after the election with you?"

"Because I'm the best newscaster in Las Vegas," she answered with a wink at the audience. "In all seriousness, I do not." And to her credit, she actually looked curious.

I nodded. "Because of your *Mythical Being of the Week* segment."

That shocked her. "Really?"

"Yep." I stared directly into the camera and took another deep breath. "I used to be a demon."

"I'm sorry, what?"

"I used to be a demon," I repeated. My gaze swung to hers. "When you first exposed the paranormal underworld here in Las Vegas, we weren't sure how it would go."

"We?"

For a newscaster, I was surprised she was struggling to keep up. "I have the ability to see the future." Elizabeth's eyes bugged. "I foresaw that your report was the right path for us."

"Thanks?"

"At that time, I was still a demon."

Elizabeth eyed me uneasily.

"Don't worry, I'm an angel now. That's why I look twenty years younger."

Gasps sounded from the dark of the studio. Really? *I'm an angel* gets gasps, when *I used to be a demon* didn't. Or was it that I looked twenty years younger. Hmm.

"I'm sure you're wondering why I'm disclosing all of this on live television."

"Among other questions," Elizabeth quipped. I was pleased she'd recovered. We needed her investigative skills for the next piece.

"What most normals don't know is that the head of the city council is also the head of the paranormal underworld for this region. And we have one of the top regions in the country."

I could practically see Elizabeth's mind processing and identifying more questions.

"Everything you've said on your segment, thus far, has been correct. Thank you for helping supernatural beings begin the transition to living fully in the open."

"That's the goal?"

"It is."

"Some of those beings have been pretty destructive."

"Indeed, they have. But, is it so different from a human who kills his neighbor, or a serial killer who takes out many?"

I saw the memory of the serial killing genie from a couple of months ago flash in Elizabeth's eyes. She nodded. "Supernatural beings have more… abilities at their disposal."

I shrugged. "Is it really so different from someone who has a high-powered machine gun, or highjacks a plane?"

She frowned and I held up a hand.

"My goal today is not to hash out all of the challenges of an integrated society. I simply wanted to confirm for your viewers that what you've been saying is the truth, and disclose my role in it in the past and going forward."

Elizabeth held my gaze for a second longer before turning to the camera. "There you have it. An ex-demon, current angel, now holds the dual title of head of the city council and head of the paranormal underworld. The next few months should be interesting, to say the least." She smiled a final time. "Thank you for tuning in – and know that we'll report back every step of the way on this explosive new development."

The camera shifted down, no longer in use, and Elizabeth faced me again. I ignored the murmurings I heard in the studio.

"Thank you for allowing me to be here," I said.

"Are you kidding? I just scooped the biggest story of my lifetime. Of several lifetimes," she crowed.

"I'm glad you feel that way, because I have one more thing."

"More than what you just said?" she asked with a raised eyebrow.

I grinned. "In my visions, I've seen Catherine Rodham repeatedly," I began.

"She doesn't like me so much anymore," Elizabeth admitted.

"I know, but that can change." I leaned closer to whisper. "Another supernatural being told me that Catherine has an important role to play."

"In what?" she whispered back.

"I'm not sure. I believe she's critical to what we're trying to build here."

Elizabeth's eyes gleamed. I had her hooked. "And you want my help to investigate?"

"You're the best. And, you've consistently demonstrated an open mind."

"I'm in. Let's figure out our plan." We grinned at each other.

Learn the final truths in the exciting conclusion to the Paranormal Talent Agency series!

And if you missed any of the earlier episodes, check them out before reading the conclusion…

PARANORMAL TALENT AGENCY

Lights, Camera, Action (PTA, #1)

Welcome to the Paranormal Talent Agency!

When empath Catherine Rodham moves across the country to launch the west coast arm of the Peterson Talent Agency in Las Vegas, her plan goes awry when an actress on a film she helped cast turns up murdered, leaving law enforcement stumped.

Alex Moore, a Sin City actor with a secret, wants agency representation from Catherine – and maybe something more. But everything changes after he finds himself the target of a murder investigation.

When the two team together to solve the serial murders, Alex introduces Catherine to a paranormal underworld she never knew existed. Can Catherine prove Alex's innocence before losing her heart…or her life?

PARANORMAL TALENT AGENCY

Reset to One (PTA, #2)

The Paranormal Talent Agency Saga Continues

All vampire Evie Jones desires is to enjoy her fun immortal life as an actress. Until she meets fellow actor Ryan Walter, who intrigues her with his insistence that his best friend has been framed for murder.

The appearance of her movie producer ex-husband in Sin City complicates Evie's offer to team with Ryan to find the real killer. She wants nothing to do with her ex, but he may hold the key to more than one murder.

Amid their growing attraction, and with the help of her Paranormal Talent Agency friends, can Evie and Ryan solve the murders…and find their happily ever after?

PARANORMAL TALENT AGENCY

That's a Wrap (PTA, #3)

Mid-Season Finale of the Paranormal Talent Agency

Mia Fynn, a nixie who has lived among humans for over 200 years, loves her life as a producer in Sin City. When the lead actor in her upcoming movie is murdered during a live social media video, Mia finds herself thrust into the role of detective.

Jacob Dawson, an actual Las Vegas Metro Police Department detective, would rather not have Mia's assistance. But even he can't deny the literal sparks that fly whenever they touch.

With the help of her Paranormal Talent Agency friends and one nosy television reporter, Mia scrambles to catch a killer… and reel in her own true love.

PARANORMAL TALENT AGENCY

An Unexpected Sequel (PTA, #4)

Mid-Season Premiere of the Paranormal Talent Agency

Five years ago, a desperate witch made a pact with a demon. Now Robin Landon, the owner of Landon Talent Agency, splits her time between managing the actors she represents and laboring as a demon's minion.

When Robin refuses the demon's order to kill Jackson McKee, a witch with a day job as a camera operator, she must balance her growing feelings for the intended target and evading the vengeful demon's wrath.

Out of options, Robin turns to her former nemeses with the Paranormal Talent Agency. Will their daring plan save Jackson from the demon, or will Robin lose both her chance at love and her life?

THANK YOU!

Thank you so much for supporting my work and reading this book. I truly hope you enjoyed reading it as much as I did writing it.

If you liked the book, please consider leaving a review online.

Just a few lines would be great. Reviews are not only the highest compliment you can pay to an author, they also help other readers discover and make more informed choices about purchasing books in a crowded online space. Thank you so much in advance.

If you didn't like the book or have concerns, please email me directly at
heather@heathersilvio.com

ABOUT THE AUTHOR

Heather has written fiction and nonfiction; she is also an actress and licensed psychologist. When she isn't working, she channels her inner flapper as a 1920s jazz and blues singer.

Visit http://www.heathersilvio.com for more information and to sign up for her New Releases and Appearances Newsletter.